BEGUILED

Two years after his last encounter with cynical nobleman Lord Murdo Balfour, David Lauriston accidentally meets him again in the heart of Edinburgh.

King George IV is about to make his first visit to Edinburgh and Murdo has been sent North by his politician father to represent his aristocratic family at the celebrations.

David and Murdo's last parting was painful—and on Murdo's part, bitter—but Murdo's feelings seem to have mellowed in the intervening years. So much so, that he suggests to David that they enjoy each other's company during Murdo's stay in the capital.

Despite his initial reservations, David cannot put Murdo's proposal from his mind, and soon find himself at Murdo's door—and in his arms.

But other figures from David's past are converging on the city, and as the pomp and ceremony of the King's visit unfolds around them, David is drawn into a chain of events that will threaten everything: his career, his wellbeing, and the fragile bond that, despite David's best intentions, is growing between him and Murdo.

BEGUILED

JOANNA CHAMBERS

Copyright © 2017 Joanna Chambers
2nd edition
Cover art: Natasha Snow
Editor: Linda Ingmanson
Published by Joanna Chambers
Print ISBN: 978-1548176259
Digital ISBN: 978-1-9997091-1-2

All rights reserved. This book or any portion thereof may not be used, reproduced or transmitted in any form or by any means without express written permission of the publisher.

This is a work of fiction. All characters, places and events in this book are fictitious. Any resemblance to actual persons, living or dead, or business establishments or organisations is completely coincidental.

Author's Note

This book is set in Edinburgh in Scotland in 1822 during the first visit of a British monarch to Scotland in almost two centuries. The monarch in question was King George IV, who, after a long period as Prince Regent, had finally become king following his father's death two years earlier.

George IV's visit to Edinburgh came at a time of considerable political unrest. Just two years before, a radical uprising by disaffected Scottish weavers (featured in Book One of this trilogy, *Provoked*) had been brutally crushed, resulting in several executions and numerous transportations. As for George IV, he was not a popular king. Profligate and self-indulgent, the King was the subject of regular public criticism, particularly over his attempt to end his marriage to Caroline of Brunswick and her subsequent death in 1821.

These circumstances might fairly be viewed as giving rise to little hope of a harmonious royal visit, and yet, with the help of the "Wizard of the North"—novelist Sir Walter Scott—the Scottish visit ended up being a triumph of patriotism. Moreover, the pageantry invented by Sir Walter Scott created, and cemented in the public consciousness, a new and romantic vision of Scotland and its "traditions", which live on to this day. In using these events as the backdrop to this story, I must acknowledge a debt to John Prebble's masterly account of King George's visit, *The King's Jaunt*. Prebble's account of the political and social backdrop to the King's visit and the numerous events and entertainments that took place during the King's fortnight-long stay was invaluable. Any flights of imagination contained in this book, such as the King's inelegant—and entirely invented—stumble in Holyrood Palace, as well as any inadvertent inaccuracies, are entirely my own.

~ JC

Chapter One

Thursday, 1ˢᵗ August, 1822
The Advocates' Library, Parliament House, Edinburgh, Scotland

David Lauriston wasn't so immersed in his reading of Viscount Stair's *Institutions* that he didn't notice how stiff his neck had grown from bending over the massive volume, but he kept reading anyway.

> *"The Affection of the Property and Chastity of Women, and Animosity and Jealousie that ariseth in Men naturally upon the Breach thereof, doth evince, that by Law of Nature, every man ought to content himself with his own Wife and Women ought not to be common; for as no man can endure the communication of his own, so it must necessarily follow, that he should not encroach on another's Property."*

That was all very well, David thought, but where did it leave his latest client, Annie Findlay? The victim of a bigamist who had died intestate, leaving her with nothing but household debts and a baby to raise, neither Annie nor the child had any claim on his sizeable estate.

Perhaps, David thought, the claim would better be raised by Annie's father? A claim against John Kerr's estate for the cost of looking after Annie and the child? He made a quick note of that thought and returned to his reading.

"Working hard, Lauriston?"

David jerked his head up, making his interrogator chuckle.

"Chalmers," he said, huffing out a laugh before adding in a faintly panicked tone, "Good lord, what time is it?"

"Half past four," Chalmers answered, lowering himself slowly into the chair on the other side of David's desk. He smiled, but his expression was tight with pain, and David felt a pang of concern for his mentor. Chalmers had been unwell in the spring and still wasn't recovered. He seemed permanently tired and had lost weight, his plump jowls turning into loose bags of skin that hung from his jaw, giving him a mournful appearance.

"Have you time for a word about the quarry case?" Chalmers asked.

"I have to get to the tailor before five," David said, "but I've a few minutes." Generally David worked side by side with Chalmers on their cases, but the quarry case was one that had come in when Chalmers was bedridden, and David had ended up doing the lion's share of work on it.

"I won't take up your time. It's just that Baxter approached me a short while ago. He wants a word—about settling, I think. I wondered if you would speak to him? Tomorrow would be fine."

David darted a curious glance at Chalmers. He'd worked with the man on quite a few cases over the last two years, and the one thing Chalmers never delegated was settlement negotiation, a skill in which he was unsurpassed. David knew he should be pleased to be trusted with this task, but concern for the older man outweighed any pleasure he'd otherwise have felt.

"Yes, that's fine," he said mildly. "I'll look him up in the morning. Any particular approach you'd like me to take?"

"You're better placed to decide than I," Chalmers said. "You've run the case on your own, and you know it inside out. I don't know it well enough to comment."

"Of course you do. We spoke about it just the other day—"

Chalmers held up his hand to stop David, giving him a stern look. "Please, don't pretend. We both know I've let you do all the work. So much so that there's practically nothing I can charge the client a fee for."

"Don't underestimate the power of your reputation," David replied, half-serious, half-teasing. "That's what you told me when we began working together, do you remember? They pay for the name." David grinned and Chalmers gave a return smile, but it was wan, and it disappeared altogether when he braced himself to stand, his expression tightening with an expectation of pain.

David stretched out a hand and laid it on the other man's forearm. "Are you all right? You seem a little tired—is there anything I can take off your shoulders?"

Chalmers tried to make his smile reassuring, but somehow it just made him look sad. "I'm fine," he said. "I just miss having Elizabeth and Catherine at home. And being ill didn't help, of course."

"You shouldn't overtax yourself. You need to get well."

"I'm better than I was. Though I'll admit, I couldn't have coped without you. You've become my right-hand man, lad. And I'm very grateful to you. You do know that, don't you?"

David shook his head, embarrassed. "It's been no hardship. You know I wanted the work. Needed it, actually."

"Don't play down what you've done. I know the hours you've put in, lad. I know how much you lifted off me." Chalmers sat back, pasting a better smile on his face and squaring his shoulders, trying to throw off the melancholy that was his constant companion these days. "So, what's so important that you need to be at the tailor by five?"

David took the hint. The serious discussion was over. He assumed a disgusted expression, more for Chalmers's amusement than anything else. "A fitting for some new clothes for the King's visit. The Dean's determined no one will show up the faculty. Apparently my usual sober clothing won't do—I've to be decked out in patriotic blue and white."

The whole of Edinburgh had been at fever pitch these last weeks over the proposed visit of King George—the first visit by a monarch to Scotland since Charles the Second. Initially little more than a rumour no one believed, it had recently been confirmed that the King would indeed be arriving in less than two weeks. Sir Walter Scott, the "Wizard of the North", whose novels the King adored, had been put in charge of the preparations for the visit, and somehow he'd managed to strike a mood of extraordinary and unprecedented patriotism amongst the city's solid and sensible burghers.

"Well, of course you must be properly attired!" Chalmers chuckled, a gallant attempt at his old good humour. "Haven't you been listening to Sir Walter? We've all to be properly costumed for the grand spectacle."

Sir Walter's lingering passion was for all things highland—albeit the highlanders of his imagination were not Jacobites but loyal British subjects who would readily bow the knee to King George. His dearest wish was to see as many of the population attired in highland dress as possible and the city's tailors, costumers and silversmiths were doing a roaring trade in kilts, sporrans and *sgian dubhs* to meet the demand. They were also doing a roaring trade in the other officially sanctioned costume of blue coat, white trousers and saltire cockade. This less showy and distinctly lowland costume was the one that David would be reluctantly adopting.

"I'm surprised you're able to get something at this stage," Chalmers said. "Someone told me the other day he couldn't even get an appointment with a tailor."

"I still might not get the clothes in time," David said glumly. "But he said he might be able to do something for me. Though if I don't make this fitting, I haven't a hope, so I'd better be off."

"Then on your way, Lauriston. We can't have you disgracing the faculty or Sir Walter, can we?"

It wanted ten minutes till five o'clock when David reached the tailor's. He was on time, thankfully, if only just. But when he pushed at the door, he found it locked.

Frowning, he rang the bell. When there was no answer, he rang it again, pulling the rope several times, but still no one came. Stepping away from the door, he went to the window and peered in through one of the small, thick panes. The shop was gloomy, but he saw the dim outline of a figure moving around.

"Hello there!" he called, rapping sharply at the glass. "Let me in, will you? I've a fitting arranged."

The figure moved forward into the light, and David could see now that it was a young lad, the tailor's assistant, presumably. A few steps from the door, he froze and looked over his shoulder towards the back of the shop, then glanced back at David and gave a helpless shrug.

Angry now, David rapped at the glass again. "I've an appointment!" he cried. "You can check—the name's David Lauriston. Mr. Riddell knows all about it."

The boy gave another shrug, his expression apologetic, then scuttled off. Was he going to see Mr. Riddell? Or was he just escaping?

Damn. David hadn't a hope of getting a suit made to Sir Walter's ridiculous specifications if Mr. Riddell didn't see him today.

He rapped the door sharply with his knuckles and rang the bell again, but after several minutes of this, it was beginning to look hopeless. Furious, he turned from the door, ready to stalk off, when the scrape of a key in the lock made him turn back.

The door opened, and a boy's anxious face poked out. "Mr. Lauriston?"

David stepped forward. "Yes."

"You're to come in, sir, please." The boy opened

the door a little more, though not by much, as though he feared a multitude might storm the gates.

With an exasperated sigh, David stepped past him, frowning to find the shop floor empty.

"Where is Mr. Riddell?"

"He's in the back, sir," the boy whispered, "with a customer. A *lord*, sir!"

A lord. A peer who had sailed in and stolen David's appointment.

"Is that why the door was locked?" he demanded, frowning.

"Yes, sir. He came an hour ago wanting to order new clothes, so Mr. Riddell bade me lock up and turn anyone else away."

"Despite their appointments?"

The lad nodded and eyed the back shop nervously. "Aye, but when you kept knocking, I went back and told Mr. Riddell you wouldn't go, and the lordship, he said to let you in if you have an appointment."

"So I have the man who stole my appointment to thank for it being kept after all?" David didn't know whether to resent the man or not. "I certainly don't have your master to thank for it, do I?"

"I shouldn't have told you," the boy said, flushing. "Mr. Riddell always says I prattle on too much." He swallowed, perhaps contemplating the scold he'd get for his loose tongue.

David sighed. "I won't say anything—so long as

Mr. Riddell honours my appointment, I don't much care. But I need this new suit before the King comes."

The boy sagged with relief. "Thank you, sir. May I trouble you to take your coat off, then? Mr. Riddell asked me to start taking your measurements."

"Very well," David said and took a step towards the back shop.

"No!" the lad protested, colouring again when David turned to look at him in surprise. "There's only one room back there, and Mr. Riddell's seeing to his lordship in there. We'll have to do it here."

"In the front shop?" David said disbelieving. "Where anyone might walk in?"

"The door's locked, sir, and you only need take your coat and boots off, if you please."

"Very well." David sighed impatiently, lifting his hands to unbutton his coat.

Flashing a grateful smile, the lad scuttled off to find his measuring tape and notebook. Soon he was taking every conceivable measurement of David's body: the length of each arm, its circumference in three separate places, the breadth of his shoulders, the line that ran from his armpit to his waist. The lad had just dropped to his knees to measure David's inside leg, when the rumble of low voices, then footsteps, signalled that Mr. Riddell and his aristocratic customer had completed their business and were about to come into the front shop.

Although he was very far from undressed, David felt exposed standing in the middle of the front shop, being measured in his stockinged feet. He looked over his shoulder in the direction of the approaching men, readying himself to say something. A quip to disguise his discomfort, and perhaps to make his displeasure known: *Please excuse my state of undress; it is so difficult to find a tailor at the moment, a man has to take what he can get. Unless he is a peer, of course...*

Mr. Riddell was the first to emerge through the connecting door—short, stocky and grey-headed, a measuring tape round his neck and the lapel of his coat glittering with pins. The other man was just behind him, and when he came through the doorway, he paused, his gaze raking the room till he found David. And smiled. A big, generous smile that dimpled one of his cheeks and made his dark eyes flash with infectious good humour.

Murdo Balfour.

"Mr. Lauriston." His smile deepened. "What a pleasant surprise!"

Only then did David realise that he had frozen and that his mouth was hanging open.

"Balfour—" he said.

He was almost surprised to hear his own voice uttering the name. Or rather breathing it, disbelieving. Rooted to the spot, he stared at the other man for long moments, his heart racing.

When they'd parted, two full years ago, Balfour had kissed David so angrily, David's lip had broken and bled.

"Don't wish me happiness, damn you…"

For days after, there had been a mark. When it was gone, David had almost missed it.

"I see you're being—measured up," Balfour said, interrupting David's swirling thoughts. He managed to make the ordinary observation sound almost indecent, and infuriatingly, David felt heat invade his cheeks.

"Yes," he said shortly, feeling entirely at a disadvantage.

Balfour's smile widened, as though David had said something amusing. "Will you be long?" he asked. "Perhaps after you're finished, we could go to a tavern and you can tell me what you've been up to since I last saw you?"

David's heart kicked. "I'm not sure how long I'll be," he said. He'd intended it to come out as a refusal, but somehow he found himself glancing at the tailor questioningly.

Mr. Riddell paused for a moment, then held out his hand to his wide-eyed assistant. The boy seemed to understand what he wanted. He put his notebook in the tailor's hand and waited while the older man scanned the scribbled measurements.

"Is your gentleman having the blue and white?" Mr. Riddell asked the boy quietly.

"Yes sir."

He turned to face Balfour. "We won't be above another ten minutes, if that's acceptable to your lordship."

If it was acceptable to *his lordship*? David bristled and glared at the tailor, but Balfour rewarded him with a condescending smile.

"That sounds ideal," Balfour said. "May I wait here while you finish?"

"Of course, my lord," Mr. Riddell replied, bowing obsequiously. "Please take a seat."

Balfour did so, settling his big, elegantly clad body into a chair at the side of the room.

David opened his mouth to say something, then closed it again. He had no doubt Balfour would find David objecting to his presence in the room like a virginal maiden protecting her modesty highly amusing. And surely there would only be one or two more measurements? Perhaps a few garments to try on? It was scarcely worth arguing over, so, pressing his lips together, he nodded at the tailor's assistant.

The lad stepped forward and proceeded to take the rest of David's measurements, calling them out to Mr. Riddell who scratched them onto the notebook. Despite his awareness of the man sitting not ten feet away, David gave his attention determinedly to the tailor, keeping his gaze averted from Balfour even after Mr. Riddell bustled through to the back of the shop.

When the tailor returned, he had a loosely tacked blue coat and a white waistcoat that looked to be all but finished draped over his arm.

"I know you're in a hurry, sir," the tailor said as he displayed the garments to David. "This waistcoat should fit you, barring a stitch here and there. I made it up for another gentleman last week, but he wasn't able to pay for it. As for the coat, the pieces were cut for a much larger gentleman who died before I could make it up, God rest his soul. If you're willing to take these, I can have them made up for you with whatever else you're needing by Monday, Tuesday at the latest. If you want new ones made from scratch, it'll be a fortnight."

When David tried on the garments, he was pleased to discover that Mr. Riddell was right about the waistcoat. It was a perfect fit. The coat felt huge, but within a few minutes, Mr. Riddell had marked the necessary alterations with chalk and fixed a few pins in place. Once he was satisfied, he eased the garment carefully from David's body and handed it to his assistant, who bore it gently through to the back shop.

"I'll make a note of your order at the desk, sir," the tailor said, his gaze flickering to Balfour, then away again. "When you're ready."

David had felt the weight of Balfour's gaze on him all through his dealings with the tailor, and sure enough, when he turned his head it was to find Balfour watching him attentively, his dark eyes glittering and his wide mouth unsmiling, for once. For an instant, their gazes locked and held and, for that instant, David couldn't breathe. He was reminded of Balfour's tendency to flout certain social rules. Especially the small, silent rules; the ones that weren't written down anywhere but were nevertheless known.

Like the rule that a man should not look at another man the way Balfour was looking at him now. Watchful. Appreciative.

The rattle of a drawer reminded David where he was, and heat flooded his cheeks again. He could imagine the rush of colour, livid against his pale complexion. The curse of the redhead. David's propensity for blushing was a source of constant consternation to him, his embarrassment over the pinkening of his cheeks only making them burn more.

Tearing his gaze from Balfour, he began to search the floor for his boots. His heart was thudding as he pulled them on, then donned his black waistcoat and coat. He almost always wore black: black trousers, black boots, even black gloves and hat. He knew he would feel odd in the blue and white of his new clothes.

The whole time David was dressing, he ignored Balfour, but he could feel the other man's attention, a prickle of awareness rippling over his skin like a caress. It was a familiar feeling, transporting him back to that time two years before, when they'd first met in the dining room of a backwater inn. To his shame, the memory made his cock stiffen in his breeches, and he had to turn away from Balfour to hide his physical reaction, spending far longer than was necessary buttoning up his coat.

Once his erection had subsided, he turned towards Mr. Riddell. The tailor stood behind the desk waiting for him, his dour face expressionless. His order book was already open, David's name and the date written there in a painstaking copperplate hand. David ordered the coat and waistcoat. Offered the choice of white or nankeen trousers, he chose one of each. He shook his head when the man offered new shirts, stockings, a low-crowned hat, all of which items he already had, thankfully. He took a cockade, though, in the requisite blue and white. The saltire colours, as prescribed by Sir Walter. He felt silly ordering such a patriotic thing in front of Balfour, but the Dean had let him know in no uncertain terms what was expected of him.

"Will that be all, sir?" Mr. Riddell asked at last.

"Yes, thank you," David replied, trying not to wince when the total was read—just shy of seven pounds of hard-earned fees. Daylight robbery! Thrown away on a suit of clothes he didn't even want.

He paid a deposit of two pounds and arranged to call in again on Monday afternoon. It occurred to him that the King might even have arrived in Scotland by then—he'd have his patriotic clothes just in time.

When he turned back to Balfour, the other man was standing and donning his hat.

"Are you ready for ale now?"

"I'd rather have a dram."

Balfour quirked a brow at him. "I'm sure that can be arranged."

Chapter Two

For a heavy man, the innkeeper of the Tolbooth Tavern had a dainty touch.

He came out from behind the bar when they entered and ushered them to a table in one of the windowed alcoves with a graceful sweep of his meaty arm. When Balfour requested whisky—inviting the man to take a dram for himself—he brought them a jug of the good stuff and three tiny pewter dram cups. Placing the cups in a neat, precise line on the table, he poured a measure of whisky into each, before picking up his own between a sausagey finger and thumb.

"To yer very good health, sirs," he toasted them. With a flick of his hand, he threw back his dram in one gulp, then, with a polite nod, left them to their business.

David watched Balfour raise one of the other cups to his lips, his eyes closing with pleasure as he took a sip. When he opened them, he smiled and admitted, "That's my first taste of whisky in a long while."

"I remember you saying you only drink whisky in

Scotland," David replied. "And that the first dram is always the best."

Balfour gave a laugh. "You have a good memory. And yes, there's nothing quite like the first taste of something, is there? Though seasoned pleasures have their place too."

Balfour always had been able to make the most innocent phrases sound rich with promise. David lifted his own dram to hide his sudden discomfiture and swallowed the contents. The taste of metal from the cup was sharp on his tongue. Then the fire of the whisky bit, and its smoke unfurled more slowly in his mouth.

"You were surprised to see me," Balfour observed. "At the tailor's."

"Of course," David replied. "Weren't you? To see me?"

Balfour's cheek dimpled as his smile curved deeply. David remembered that smile. It made Balfour's very masculine, darkly handsome face appear suddenly and disarmingly boyish.

"Well, I had the benefit of prior warning," Balfour said. "Obviously I knew when I came to Edinburgh there was a chance I'd see you. Even so, when the boy at the tailor's interrupted my fitting with the news that a Mr. Lauriston was rapping at the window demanding to be seen and wouldn't go away, I was a little taken aback. Riddell told him to ignore you, but I couldn't let you slip through my fingers, so I bade him let you in."

David's chest felt suddenly tight. He was amazed at how calm his voice sounded when he replied, "Just as well, or I'd've missed my appointment."

Balfour gave another soft laugh. "Riddell was very accommodating."

"To you," David supplied dryly.

"You can't blame him. It's good business sense. Now he can boast an aristocrat as a customer."

"He's probably had aristocrats beating down his door all week. I've never seen so many people in the city," David replied. "They're sleeping in tents on the Calton Hill."

"So I heard." Balfour shook his head in wonderment. "I'd never have thought my fellow Scots would've been so excited by a visit from a Hanoverian king. It's not *that* long since the '45."

"It's very odd," David agreed. "But somehow the people have been convinced that we Scots are the most loyal subjects the King has in all the British Isles."

Balfour shook his head again and leaned back in his chair, his dram cup sitting patiently in front of him, barely sipped. When David glanced at his own cup, he found it empty. He couldn't even remember drinking it all. He found he wanted another and clenched his hands under the table to stop himself reaching for the jug.

"So why have you come back here?" he asked after a brief silence. "Are you playing a part in the festivities?"

"A bit part. I'm representing the family—excuse me, the *clan*. One must observe Sir Walter's Celtifications. To pass muster as acting head of the clan, I've had to be fitted out in the finest highland dress—I've spent a fortune on tartan and eagle feathers over the last few weeks."

David chuckled, then asked, "Why isn't your father here?"

"Oh, Father's far too busy with the Verona business to come up—that's exactly what the government wants the King to keep his nose *out* of. It had to be me or my brother, and since the King's not too fond of my brother, it fell to me."

David recalled Balfour speaking of his dislike of his father's manipulations. "I'm surprised to find you doing your father's bidding so willingly," he remarked.

Balfour just shrugged. "I was planning to come up to Scotland anyway. Once this fiasco's over with, I'm going up to Perthshire to my own estate. I've not managed up since I bought it, and I plan to stay for a couple of months at least."

"I remember you talking about buying an estate in Perthshire—is it the same one? The one with the beautiful views?"

"The very same. And the views *are* wonderful, but

I've a thousand and one problems to resolve. The previous owner seems to have had disputes with every man within fifty miles, every one with a history as long as your arm. It was bad enough when I first bought the place—then, a few months ago, the estate manager took another position and it's become ten times worse. I need to spend a good while up there to get it turned about."

David laughed softly. "Mr. Chalmers told you to beware beautiful views."

"Yes, but I still think they're worth it. The best things in life invariably require the most effort, don't you think?" Balfour lounged in his chair, his long legs stretched out before him, the very picture of confident masculinity. "Wasn't it you who once told me that life isn't all about pleasure?"

David swallowed. "I don't remember," he said, looking away.

That was a lie. He remembered every part of that particular conversation—that last conversation—as though each word had been branded on his flesh.

"If life isn't about pleasure or happiness, what is it about? Tell me, Lauriston, so I can learn from your great wisdom."

"I think it's about being true to yourself…"

This time, David did reach for the jug, sloppily topping Balfour's glass to the brim, then his own, and lifting the cup to his lips to take a gulp of the spirit.

"I see you still like to drink," Balfour remarked dryly, adding, "and you look as though you still forget to eat. I take it you ignored the last bit of advice I gave you?"

"What advice?"

"To get yourself a wife to take care of you. Specifically, that young woman who was so enamoured of you. Miss Chalmers, wasn't it?"

David realised that Balfour couldn't know how sensitive a subject that was, but he couldn't stop himself snapping, "Of course I ignored you. What did you expect?"

Balfour took another small sip from his cup before he replied. "Just that. You were very clear in that last conversation, when you told me you would never marry."

"It was more of an argument than a conversation, if I remember correctly," David replied tightly.

For a while, Balfour didn't say anything. Then he sighed and said, "Later—when I returned to London—I came to regret the way we parted. My anger especially."

That admission took David by surprise. "Why were you so angry?"

Balfour fixed his gaze on the scarred wooden table, one hand idly playing with his dram cup. "You took a huge risk that night when you stepped in front of MacLennan's pistol. I was angry at you for risking your life—especially to save my worthless cousin."

"Euan would never have shot me," David said.

Balfour gave a bark of humourless laughter. "He was this close," he said, holding his thumb and finger half an inch apart.

David just shook his head. Impossible to explain that his decision to step in front of that pistol had been to save Euan, not Hugh Swinburne. And that when Euan had run away rather than shoot David, David's faith in the lad had, thankfully, been vindicated.

"That wasn't the only reason you were angry," he said.

Balfour glanced at him, then gave a defeated sigh. "No," he admitted. "I found you…provoking. Your views were so earnest, so uncompromising. All or nothing. I could tell you despised me for saying I intended to marry at some stage."

"I didn't *despise* you," David protested. "In fact, I made a point of saying that I could only speak for me and my conscience."

"It wasn't just that," Balfour said with a wry look. "Yes, I was shocked by your reckless act that night. And yes, it bothered me to feel judged by you. But when I thought about why I was so angry, I realised it was…fear for you."

"Fear?"

"I could see how easily it could destroy you—this passion you have, this commitment to your principles.

You can't seem to walk away from it, even when it endangers you. I couldn't believe anyone could have so little instinct for self-preservation. It made me angry." He paused. "But as I said, I regretted that, later. Wished we could have parted on better terms. The time we spent together before that was—interesting."

David didn't know what to say. His throat felt as if it had closed up entirely. He'd felt regret too. Regret for allowing Balfour to seduce him. Regret for opening himself up to the desolation that had swamped him in the months that followed that last, bitter conversation.

"Was Miss Chalmers disappointed?" Balfour asked, changing the subject abruptly. "I rather had the impression she had set her cap at you."

He was right—Elizabeth had set her cap at him, and David hadn't even realised. Oh, he'd known she liked him, but it was months after Balfour went back to London that David had finally, far too slowly, caught on. And then there was that awful day, the day David asked to speak to her in private. He'd wanted to tell her, gently, that he intended never to marry. Only she'd misunderstood and thought he meant to propose. That had been a painful conversation, and when he'd left her, he'd been weighed down by a burden of guilt that had only begun to ease when she'd married, quite suddenly, a few months later.

"Miss Chalmers is now Lady Kinnell," he told Balfour calmly. "She lives in Galloway on her new husband's estate. So she has done far better for herself than if she'd married me."

"She is married to *Sir Alasdair Kinnell?*" Balfour replied. An expression of dislike arrested his handsome face. "Surely not? She's much too sweet for the likes of him. His first wife was an unhappy girl. I wondered if she did away with herself to get away from the brute."

David felt himself pale. "You know him?"

"I went to school with him. He liked to terrorise the younger boys, of whom I, unfortunately, was one. For a time anyway."

The thought that Elizabeth may have married a man who would mistreat her made David feel sick. Made the old feelings of guilt stir in him again. He'd been so relieved when he'd heard of her engagement to Kinnell, pleased that she'd found a husband so obviously more eligible than himself.

He realised Balfour was watching him and shoved his disturbing thoughts aside to be examined later.

"What about you?" he said to deflect Balfour's attention. "Have you taken your own advice?"

"Have I married, do you mean? No, not yet."

Not yet.

"But you intend to."

Balfour stared at David for a long moment. Was he remembering their last conversation again? When Balfour had confirmed his intention to eventually marry, while continuing to enjoy male lovers at his whim.

"I intend to wed at some stage, yes," Balfour said finally.

An entirely predictable statement, that. David felt suddenly flat.

Why was he sitting here? Why had he agreed to come here with Balfour in the first place? He should've declined the man's invitation and gone home to tackle the work sitting on his desk.

Throwing back the rest of his whisky, he set his cup down on the table, very quietly and precisely, then glanced up and smiled pleasantly. "Well," he said. "It was good to see you, Balfour, but I really must be going. I've a lot of work to do this evening."

He scraped his chair back, moving to rise. Before he could do so, Balfour leaned forward and laid his hand on David's forearm.

"Wait a moment," he said. A faint frown drew his brows together. Those brows were dark against his pale skin; his eyes were too, black as ink. It was a wild, dramatic combination, the pale skin, the dark eyes. This close, David recalled, pointlessly, what it felt like to look into those eyes when they glittered with desire. Memory flooded him; his cock throbbed.

David jerked back, pulling his arm from Balfour's grip even as he subsided back into his chair, ruining his pretence at cheerful unconcern. "I can't stay," he muttered. "I have things to do. Work."

"I just—I need to tell you something," Balfour persisted. "Though you may know already, I suppose."

"What is it?"

"Your friend is in town," Balfour said. "Euan MacLennan."

David didn't bother to hide his astonishment. "Euan?" he said at last. "Are you quite sure?"

Balfour regarded him calmly for a long moment. "You didn't know." It was a statement rather than a question, and his still, quiet face gave nothing away of what he made of the conclusion he'd reached.

"No. I haven't seen him for a long time. Not since the night we spoke of earlier."

On hearing that confirmation, something in Balfour seemed to relax, a faint tension in his shoulders easing. He leaned back in his chair again. "Have you any idea why he might be here? Has he written to you?"

David didn't reply straightaway. A vague sense of unease settled over him. At last he said, carefully, "As I said, I've not seen him—not for two years. Nor have I heard from him in that time."

He watched Balfour's reaction more carefully this time, but the man never gave much away, and he didn't now.

"That's good to hear." Balfour seemed to consider for a moment before adding, "You don't want to be associated with him."

David frowned. "Why would you say that?"

Balfour looked up at the ceiling, regarding its murky gloom for several seconds before he looked back at David. "I shouldn't be telling you this, but amongst the visitors to Edinburgh, there are a number of men—some of them Peel's official men, some less official—who've been tasked with keeping an eye on certain unsavoury characters."

Peel. Balfour meant Sir Robert Peel, David realised. The Home Secretary.

"Unsavoury characters? Euan's an 'unsavoury character'?"

"In Peel's eyes, yes. He's on a list I've seen."

"A list," David said slowly. "What kind of list?"

"A list of men Peel wants to keep his beady eye on during the King's visit. MacLennan's a known radical. I don't know what he's been doing precisely these last two years, but I gather there's a file on him in Peel's office. There are others on the list too, all kinds of potential troublemakers—anyone who might be a threat to the King and who's known to have travelled north."

"Why were you shown this list?" David asked, suspicion pricking at him.

Balfour shrugged. "My father's a minister of government. I am his representative on this visit. As such, I've been made privy to certain information."

"And why," David continued, watching Balfour

carefully, "are you telling me about it?"

Balfour didn't answer straightaway. He picked up his cup and drank from it. Set it down again and sighed. Looked out the window.

Then, with his gaze still averted, he said quietly, "If you're seen with MacLennan, it might affect you. Guilt by association. A suspicious rumour about your political leanings, and you may find your career suffers. I wouldn't want that to happen to you. I wanted to…warn you."

There was something melancholy about Balfour as he spoke, something sad about the slightly distant look he wore as he stared out the window. Then he turned back and gave a quick quirk of a smile. Bright and unconvincing. "And now I've been indiscreet enough. Please don't mention what I've told you to anyone else, will you?"

David shook his head slowly. "No. No, I won't. Though frankly, I doubt Euan will seek me out, given how we parted."

Euan had been furious at David for depriving him of his chance of revenge.

There was a brief silence when they looked at each other, really looked. For the first time, David saw, not the amused and elegant exquisite that was Lord Murdo Balfour, but another man. A man with secret desires and perhaps secret griefs too.

Balfour was the first to look away. "I'll let you go,

then," he said lightly. "Let you get back to your work. I know how important it is to you, and you must have a great deal to do if you're contemplating spending the evening on it."

If there was a trace of sarcasm in there, David chose to ignore it. He stood, and Balfour rose from his chair too, readying himself to bid David farewell.

God, but this was civilised. At their last meeting, two long years ago, they'd exchanged a barrage of harsh words. A kiss that left blood in David's mouth.

I came to regret the way we parted...

A slow smile tugged at Balfour's lips as they stood there, facing one another. The smile was so unexpected, it tripped David up for a moment.

"It was good to see you," Balfour said softly, the tone of his deep voice uncharacteristically sincere, no trace of his usual mockery.

David nodded. Swallowed. "And you," he said at last. He offered his hand, and, after a moment, Balfour took it. The man's grip was warm and steady, and it grounded something in David.

"I would...like to see you again," Balfour said then, his voice low.

David didn't know what to say. He searched Balfour's face and saw he was serious. "I don't know—" he began. He recalled too easily the long, melancholy winter that had followed their last parting.

"You don't need to give me an answer," Balfour

replied. "You know where my house is. Come anytime. I'll be in town for the next month at least. I'll instruct my servants to admit you, even if I am not there."

He released David's hand. Their arms fell to their respective sides, and they were separate again.

"I'll think about it," David said, after a pause.

He suspected he'd do little else.

He nodded at Balfour once; then he turned and walked out the tavern.

The door closed behind him. He lingered for a moment to turn his coat collar up against the drizzling rain before he began the short stroll to his rooms in the Lawnmarket.

As he paced up the street, he heard Balfour's words in his mind again.

"I would like to see you again."

I would like to see you again.

They were such commonplace words.

Such commonplace words to make him feel so utterly hollowed out.

Chapter Three

Monday, 12th August, 1822

"Why did I let you persuade me into this, Ferguson?" David grumbled as he searched his pantry for a platter to hold the fruit cake that his friend had brought.

David's little kitchen table was already crammed in preparation for his guests' arrival: cold roast fowl, sliced mutton, a plate of little savoury pies that his maidservant had fetched at near dawn this morning along with gingerbread and scones. And now a rich fruit cake. It would be a feast.

Donald Ferguson laughed, his round, merry face making David smile despite himself. "Because you've the best view of the procession of anyone I know, Lauriston. And because I shamed you into it, of course."

Donald Ferguson was a young advocate whose late father, a judge, had been a particular friend of Chalmers's. Chalmers had sent some work the younger man's way, and Ferguson had repaid him by taking one of his daughters off his hands. Catherine Chalmers was now Catherine Ferguson.

The Fergusons were a well-suited pair, David thought. Both good-humoured and prone to laughter, though Catherine's sense of humour was drier than Donald's.

Ferguson called almost every man in the faculty friend. Why he bothered seeking out the company of David, who was serious, studious and downright unsociable, was unfathomable to David. But for some reason, the man had decided to make a friend of him, insisting on having David over to his and Catherine's small home to dine with them at least once a week, as well as dragging David away from his desk in the library at some point most days, whether to beg for David's advice on a case, or for his company at a tavern or coffee house.

When David had complained to Chalmers of Ferguson diverting him from his work, the older man had merely laughed.

"It's just as well he does," Chalmers said. "Someone has to remind you to eat."

Reminding David to eat was one thing; persuading him to invite a dozen guests into his brand-new rooms at an absurdly early hour of the day to watch the "Carrying of the Regalia of Scotland" from the castle to Holyrood Palace was quite another. It was true, though, that his apartments were ideal for the purpose.

Situated close to the castle on the Lawnmarket and high up on the third floor, David's front windows were a perfect location from which to watch the procession make its way to and from the castle. Already, the street below was brimming with spectators.

"It's not even a real ceremony," David grumbled as he transferred the cake Ferguson had brought onto the plate he'd unearthed. "Just some made-up pageantry of Sir Walter's."

"Oh, don't be such a misery." Ferguson laughed. "People love Sir Walter's pageantry. They love to feel they're part of a rich tradition—what's the harm in that?"

David scowled. "And what's wrong with the truth? Why do people want to believe in all this nonsense?"

"It's not *complete* nonsense."

David shifted some of the plates on the table around to create a space for the cake. "Near enough. They only found the so-called 'Regalia of Scotland' a few years ago. And it's certainly never before been transported from one end of the High Street to the other by a parcel of aristocrats in tartan who couldn't find their collective way to Holyrood Palace without written directions."

Ferguson chuckled. "Well, there's a first time for every tradition," he said. "And you can't deny the people are enjoying it."

"No, I can't," David sighed. The public enthusiasm

for the King's visit bewildered him. He'd never have thought in a thousand years his fellow Scots could be whipped up into such eager hysteria. But then the architect of the visit, Sir Walter Scott, was an old hand at creating dramatic fictions, wasn't he? And as Ferguson said, the people were loving the pageantry, even if it was a complete fabrication.

"Considering how much you dislike all this," Ferguson continued good-naturedly, "it's good of you to invite so many fellows up to share your view. The rest of us shall certainly be glad of it."

David merely arched a brow at that, and Ferguson had the grace to laugh, his cheeks pinkening. They both knew that the invitations, to a number of other advocates and solicitors and their wives, had been prompted by Ferguson.

"Oh, and I should mention, you will have one more guest," Ferguson continued a little shamefacedly. "I hope you don't mind. I should've said earlier."

David sighed. "Who is it this time?"

"Catherine's sister Elizabeth is in town with her husband. We popped in on our way over this morning—Kinnell wasn't in; apparently he has other business to attend to today—but Catherine urged Elizabeth to come along. She felt sure you wouldn't mind."

David softened. "No, of course not. I shall be pleased to see Lady Kinnell again."

More than pleased, actually. Ever since Balfour's unpleasant comments about Kinnell's supposed character, Elizabeth had been playing on his mind. David hoped that Balfour was wrong, that he'd been exaggerating about Kinnell's brutality, and that his speculation about Kinnell's first wife was merely that— speculation. He knew he wouldn't feel easy in his own mind till he had satisfied himself Elizabeth was well and happy.

"The ladies are only a few minutes behind me," Ferguson went on. "They wanted to walk up the last bit of the High Street more slowly and see some of the spectacles going on. They'll be here shortly, I expect. And the other guests won't be far behind." Ferguson cast a worried eye round the kitchen. "Don't you have anything to drink?"

"It's all in the parlour," David assured him. "There's ale and wine punch. Some lemonade too. Will that do?"

Ferguson smiled. "That sounds perfect."

David thought of the bottle of whisky he'd put away. Even amongst his fellow Scots, there'd be some disapproving looks if he started in on the hard stuff this early in the day, especially in front of ladies. Oh, why had he agreed to this ridiculous gathering?

A rap on the door interrupted his thoughts.

Ferguson strode to the door before David could make his feet move. Moments later, Catherine bounced in, all glossy curls and sparkly eyes.

"Oh, Mr. Lauriston, how very nice your rooms are!" she exclaimed, clasping her hands together. "I'd imagined some drab old bachelor apartments, but this is very cosy. And oh, do look! I have Elizabeth with me, visiting from her *estate*, if you please, in Galloway. Doesn't she look well?"

David's gaze moved over Catherine's shoulder to the small person standing behind her.

If the quality of her garments was all he judged, then yes, she looked very well indeed, in a dark blue pelisse and a high poke bonnet decorated with a long curling feather. But that was not all he saw. He saw that her face was thinner and quite pale, and that her dark eyes held, he thought, a faint shadow. Her smile too—a smile he'd always liked a great deal—was a shade dimmer.

With the old plumpness gone from her face, she was conventionally prettier than she'd been the last time he'd seen her, half a year ago. In fact, she was rather beautiful in her way. But all her *joie de vivre* had gone.

"Mr. Lauriston," she said softly. "How very nice it is to see you again." She held her hands out to him and he stepped forward, taking both of them in his own and looking down at her upturned face. He remembered the last time they'd stood as close as this. He remembered watching the glow of happiness she'd worn draining away, leaving behind an expression of bewildered hurt.

"I have no intention of taking a wife, Miss Chalmers."

Christ, he'd been clumsy. "Lady Kinnell," he said now. He searched her face for a moment, but she quickly averted her eyes and gently tugged her gloved hands out of his grasp, her dashing bonnet obscuring his view of her face as she walked past him to join her sister, who stood at the sash windows.

"Is this where we'll watch the procession from?" she asked in a brittle tone. "Goodness, what a view! We're so close to the castle, Mr. Lauriston!"

"And once we raise the windows, we'll see the whole spectacle perfectly," Ferguson pointed out, joining the ladies. "Though we'll have to take turns at the front—there're quite a few others coming."

"We passed some spectator stands set up on the street, didn't we, Lizzie?" Catherine said. "Some of them look very rickety, I think. We're much better off up here, in comfort and with ten times the view. We'll see everything from here."

David and Ferguson exchanged a grin at Catherine's girlish enthusiasm.

Within another quarter hour, David's rooms were fairly bursting at the seams. The guests arrived all at once, and as soon as the introductions were made, David and the Fergusons were run off their feet making everyone comfortable and passing round refreshments.

For the first little while, most of David's guests milled around the windows of the parlour, which gave a bird's eye view of the Lawnmarket below. David had opened the sash windows as far as possible, and the noise of the crowd outside—haphazard cheering and occasional outbreaks of bagpipe music and drums—was raucous enough that David's guests had to talk loudly to be heard.

Whilst the duties of hosting required David to overcome his natural reserve to some extent, as soon as he'd welcomed each guest and handed them a drink, he began to feel unsettled. He missed his whisky and gulped at his weak, hoppy ale as he circulated, filling his cup nearly as often as he fetched drinks for his guests.

After an hour or so, he was surprised to hear another knock at the door. He was sure all the guests had arrived and, casting his gaze around the room, verified that, yes, everyone he'd invited was here already. It must be another of Ferguson's last-minute additions.

David began to sidle his way through the knots of guests crowding his parlour, but it was slow going, and when he caught Elizabeth's gaze on the other side of the room, he was relieved when she waved and gestured that she would go to answer the door. Nodding gratefully, he continued to inch forward, trying not to press against any of the ladies.

By the time he got into the hallway, the door was open and a new, male guest had stepped into the house. A tall, broad-shouldered man who held Elizabeth's hand between his own, his fair head bowed as he listened to what she was saying. At the sound of David's footsteps, the man looked up, revealing an earnestly handsome face with which David was very familiar.

Euan MacLennan.

David abruptly halted where he stood. "Euan."

Euan met his gaze and smiled apologetically. "Hello, Davy. I'm sorry to call on you without warning. It's obviously not the best time."

It was two years since they'd last come face-to-face, on the night that David had stepped between Euan's pistol and Hugh Swinburne—or Lees, as he'd been known then—to prevent Euan becoming a murderer.

Despite confidently telling Balfour that Euan would never have shot him, he would probably never know how close Euan had come to it. Euan had desperately wanted to kill Swinburne, a government agent instrumental in having Euan's brother, Peter, transported for treason, but in the end, Euan had walked away.

Looking at him now, David had to wonder whether Euan was still angry at him for depriving him of his opportunity. The man's politely smiling face gave nothing away.

He'd changed over the last two years—filled out. Now he was positively brawny. Tall and burly, more like Peter now. Less a boy and more a man.

David made himself move forward, taking the hand the other man offered in a brief grasp. "It's been a long time," David said, his expression carefully neutral.

Euan opened his mouth to speak, but before he could do so, Elizabeth interrupted.

"I was just saying to Mr. MacLennan that he looked familiar. I take it he's a friend of yours, Mr. Lauriston?"

So, Euan had introduced himself already.

"And I was about to answer Lady Kinnell that she and I saw one another at an assembly I attended a few years ago in the Assembly Rooms. I was with you, Davy. Do you remember?" Euan turned his head to smile down at Elizabeth. "We were not formally introduced that evening. I was too embarrassed to dance or speak with any ladies. Davy spent most of the night trying to persuade me to do so, to no avail."

It bore a passing resemblance to the truth, David supposed, though his only reason for suggesting Euan dance had been to enable the lad to ask the questions that might lead him to Hugh Swinburne.

"How foolish," Elizabeth said, laughing somewhat nervously. "Well, you can make up for your past misdemeanours by joining this party and speaking with all the ladies. What do you think, Mr. Lauriston?" She glanced at David, a question in her dark gaze. For that moment, she was almost the old Elizabeth, though there was something a little withdrawn about her still.

That rare and welcome glimpse of the girl he remembered, however fleeting, distracted David, and he smiled at her, even as Balfour's warnings about being seen with Euan MacLennan resonated in his mind. Giving no hint of those thoughts, he told her, "I think it's an excellent idea." Then he turned his attention back to Euan and added, "Well, don't hover there in the doorway, come in."

Waving Elizabeth ahead, then Euan, David took up the rear himself.

"You can leave your hat on the table there," he told Euan, waving at the hall table. "Everyone's in the parlour."

"I don't want to intrude," Euan protested, though he took his hat off and set it on the table as directed.

"You're not intruding," David murmured with automatic politeness. "We're only waiting to see the procession." Even as he spoke the words, it occurred to him to wonder whether Euan was being followed, if someone, one of Peel's men, was watching them now, noting David's address down and marking him as a possible sympathiser to radical causes.

"So, how did you find me?" David asked as he led the way to the front room where the other guests were.

"I called at your old rooms, and a woman there

gave me your direction," Euan explained. "These rooms are much nicer. You must be doing well, Davy."

David glanced at the younger man, but there appeared to be no sarcasm in his tone or expression.

"I've been working hard."

"You always did," Euan replied with a smile.

David wasn't sure how to take that. "Ale?" he offered shortly.

"Ah, yes, thank you."

"Let's get you something to eat, Mr. MacLennan," Elizabeth suggested on Euan's other side. "Mr. Lauriston's table has something to tempt everyone, I'm sure."

While David fetched Euan's ale, Elizabeth led him to the sideboard where the food lay to help him select some repast. When David joined them there, he was just in time to hear Elizabeth ask, "And what is it you do, Mr. MacLennan?"

Euan put down the little meat pie he'd been about to bite into.

"I'm a journalist," he said, taking the cup David proffered with a murmur of thanks.

"A journalist?" Elizabeth repeated. "How interesting. Do you write for a particular periodical?"

For a long moment, Euan paused; then, casting a quick glance at David, he said, "You may not have heard of it. *Flint's Political Register.*"

David saw that Elizabeth had heard of it, all

right—and who had not? Her dark eyes widened fractionally before she nodded.

Flint's was a London paper, a radical periodical. With twice the subscribers of Blackwood's, it was highly popular amongst the lower classes, and hated by the government.

"Yes, I've heard of it," Elizabeth said carefully. "But I thought—I thought it had been closed down." She seemed more curious than condemnatory.

"It's been closed down several times actually," Euan replied. "Every time they close us down, we start up again. Tom Gilmour, who founded it, has been in prison almost a twelvemonth. His wife managed to keep it going for a while after he went in. Then she was jailed too, just last month. Her sister has taken up the mantle for now, and if—or when—she is arrested, the rest of us will keep it going. The people need—"

He broke off. Perhaps he'd noticed David's gaze flickering around them, checking if any of the other guests were listening. When their eyes met, his expression was part mortification, part defiance. "Sorry. I shouldn't—I'm an uninvited guest…"

The brief, tense silence was broken by Elizabeth. "I hope you're not apologising on my account," she said. "I've never met a journalist before. Are you in Edinburgh to write a story?"

That adept little question—a change of direction rather than subject—was typically astute of Elizabeth, and Euan answered gratefully.

"Yes. I'll be writing a series of articles on the King's visit to Scotland, actually." He didn't need to add that the tone of those articles would be quite different from the fawning flattery of some of the more respectable periodicals. If the articles were to be published by *Flint's Political Register*, they would be decidedly republican in tone.

"Ah, now I see why you visited Mr. Lauriston today," Elizabeth said with a little twinkle in her eye. "You are no better than the rest of us here, begging a bit of a view."

Euan laughed, even as he appeared discomfited by her teasing, shifting a little on his feet. "In my defence, I wasn't expecting the view to be quite so good as this. Davy's come up in the world since last I saw him."

Before David could decide whether the words were a compliment or an accusation, Catherine's voice rang out over the murmured conversations in the room.

"Oh, do come and see, everyone! They're moving at last!"

David's guests rushed to the window of the parlour. It was plain that it would be impossible for everyone to get a view, notwithstanding that it was a double window and the ladies had obligingly removed their bonnets.

"I've a smaller window in my study that a few of us could watch from," David suggested to the people craning their necks at the back. "Follow me."

He walked down the short length of the hall and opened the door to his study at the end, holding it open for the small group that had followed him: Elizabeth, Euan and a married couple, the Beggs.

"Oh good! We shall end up having a much better view with just five of us!" Mrs. Begg said happily.

"Ladies to the front, I should think," Begg said, raising the sash. His wife rushed forward, giggling with excitement, and he stationed himself behind her as though he were her personal bodyguard, turning to Elizabeth to add, "There's plenty of room at the front, my lady. We gentlemen shall stand at the back."

Elizabeth shuffled forward, seeming uncomfortable. For an instant, David wondered why; then he didn't have to wonder. She gave away the reason all by herself, with the hand that went to her neck to tug her stiff collar up a little higher. He wondered if he'd have noticed what she sought to hide if she hadn't made that betraying little gesture. As it was, he couldn't help but notice the dark, purplish bruises there, distinctly placed by a hand, the visible bruise-smudges of the fingers on one side and the print of a thumb on the other. It must have been a cruel grip—and recent—to leave such livid marks.

David saw that Euan had plainly seen the marks too—he was frowning. Euan glanced at David, partly as though to check that he too had seen what looked like evidence of abuse, and partly as though seeking an explanation. David shook his head in demonstration of his ignorance, but he couldn't help remembering Balfour's words about Elizabeth's husband as his eyes were drawn again to the back of her neck.

Such a little neck. Though women had never roused his passions, he was not unaffected by them. He appreciated the tender curves of them, the promise they held of succour and safety and home. Looking at Elizabeth's bruised flesh brought David's protective instincts to the fore and made him feel sick to his very stomach. How could a man put violent hands on a woman?

On Elizabeth, of all women?

Chapter Four

It took forty-five minutes for the procession to work its way past David's windows on its way up to the castle.

The Beggs enjoyed it to the full. Especially Mrs. Begg, who *oohed* and *ahhed*, who pointed out which clans each contingent of highlanders was from—she appeared to have memorised all the tartans—and breathlessly intoned the names of the more important personages as they passed, particularly the mounted clan chiefs in their full regalia.

"Look at Sir Evan MacGregor," she breathed as the MacGregor clan swept by in a torrent of scarlet. "Have you ever seen anyone so handsome in all your life, Lady Kinnell?"

"Present company excepted, no," Elizabeth replied, a smile in her voice.

"Oh well, of course!" Mrs. Begg replied, giggling. "Kenneth knows I esteem him above all others, don't you, my love? But Sir Evan's costume is just so *dashing*."

"I shall have to purchase one just like it," Mr. Begg replied. "Can you imagine me, Lauriston, addressing the Lord President in tartan and eagle feathers?"

"I would pay good money to see it," David said, and everyone laughed.

"And there is Lord Murdoch Balfour," Mrs. Begg went on. "Do you see him, Kenneth? On the black horse?"

David's heart began to beat in his throat at the sound of that name. It was almost a fortnight since he'd run into the man at the tailor shop, and every day he thought of their last conversation.

"You know where my house is. Come anytime..."

He thought about that invitation, every day. But he hadn't gone. The memory of how he'd felt two years before, after they'd parted, lingered still. The blackness that had descended on him afterwards. The long, endless downhill from the mountain. Down and down.

He feared to tread that black descent again.

From the corner of his eye, he saw Euan studying him—Euan recognised Balfour's name, of course—but David didn't turn his head. He kept looking forward, letting his gaze roam over the riders below, until, at last, he picked out Balfour, tall and elegant on his midnight steed.

David was as sceptical as it was possible to be about this ceremony. He'd watched hundreds of troops pass to the patriotic sound of bagpipes and drums without feeling the slightest bit moved. But when he saw Balfour, dressed far less flamboyantly than Sir Evan MacGregor, in dark-green-and-blue tartan, he felt a stirring in his breast for the first time all day.

It wasn't with patriotism, though. It was with a far more personal feeling.

"Oh, he's like Young Lochinvar," Mrs. Begg breathed, and they all laughed again, David too. And it *was* funny, except…except that she was right.

So faithful in love, and so dauntless in war
There never was knight like the young Lochinvar…

Inwardly, David groaned. Was he a lassie to be thinking such nonsense?

He'd spent the last two years trying to forget Lord Murdo Balfour, certain he'd never see the man again. It had been over a year before he'd given in to his old weakness, scared that touching another man, or being touched, would stir up memories he wanted to forget.

That fear had been unfounded, as it happened. His first lapse hadn't reminded him of Balfour at all, nor any of the few times after that. Those furtive, anonymous encounters had borne no relation to being with Balfour. David scarcely spoke to any of those men, scarcely even looked at them. He'd certainly never looked at any of them as he was looking at Balfour now, with his heart kicking a determined tattoo in his chest and his breath coming shallow and quick at the mere sight of him, down on the street below on his black steed.

"You know where my house is."

"Goodness me, it *is* Lord Murdo!" Elizabeth said then. "Do you remember him, Mr. Lauriston?" She turned her head and caught his eye, forcing him to reluctantly look away from Balfour's departing figure. "You dined with him at my father's house once. Do you recall?"

"Ah—yes, I believe I do," David confirmed.

"Do you know," Euan said in a tone that held an audible note of amusement, "I think I recognise him too."

David glanced at Euan, a slight frown drawing his brows together in warning—Euan was perfectly well aware of Lord Murdo Balfour's identity. Balfour had been with David that night two years before, had bargained with Euan after David's reckless intervention. There was no way he could have forgotten him.

Euan feigned puzzlement, a finger on his lips. "Was he possibly at the assembly we talked about earlier? The one Lady Kinnell was at?"

David stayed silent, letting Euan know he wasn't happy, but Elizabeth interjected, unwittingly rescuing the younger man.

"I believe he *was* at that assembly, Mr. MacLennan. I remember I had to dance with him, and it was terribly nerve-racking! Mother had persuaded herself he was looking for a wife, and she was being utterly impossible that night."

"Looking for a fancy son-in-law, was she?" Mr. Begg asked with jolly tactlessness.

Elizabeth's smile faded a little, but she answered him with a show of good humour that didn't quite reach her eyes. "Yes. Well, she got her wish in the end. Though not with Lord Murdo Balfour."

She turned back to face the window then, her shoulders and back tense, and the thumbprint bruise at the nape of her neck livid. David glanced at Euan, who looked grim. Of course, he'd been looking fairly grim throughout the whole procession. It was obvious to anyone who cared to look that he didn't find the spectacle as stirring as David's other guests. Perhaps he saw it as a demonstration of the power of the state—all that military might being displayed in honour of the monarch of the United Kingdoms of England, Scotland, Wales and Ireland.

David's view of the procession was probably closer to Euan's than to that of the patriotic Beggs. Yet he'd hosted this celebration. Brought in food and wine and played the part of a loyal subject of the King. Well, he was loyal, wasn't he? Certainly in deed, if not in thought. He was a respectable man, part of the machinery that upheld the rule of law, even when he tried to fight its effect. Like when he'd represented

Euan's brother. He'd tried his damnedest, within the bounds of the law, to prevent Peter MacLennan being transported, but it hadn't been enough.

What a man could do within the law was rarely enough, and that was the hell of it.

Once the procession was over, and while the formal ceremony to hand over the Regalia was being conducted in the castle, David's small party returned to the other guests in the parlour. David circulated the room, offering his guests more refreshments. While he topped the ladies' glasses with wine punch, Ferguson refreshed the men's ale, and Catherine replenished some of the empty plates on the sideboard from the kitchen.

David's guests were jolly by now, some even becoming a little silly. Hardly surprising when they were tippling before noon. Despite his sociable demeanour, David didn't feel jolly, though. He felt too sober, untouched by the ale he'd drunk and out of step with his guests' merriness, and it wasn't just the alcohol or his distaste for the pageantry bothering him.

Once David had been round all the other guests, he approached Euan and Elizabeth. They stood a little apart, talking together, their heads bent close. He felt, oddly, like an intruder as he drew near.

"Would you like some more lemonade, Lady Kinnell? Or more ale for you, Mr. MacLennan?"

They looked up simultaneously, both of them

seeming surprised to see him standing there for an instant before they each began to refuse his offer, their words tumbling together then petering out into awkward silence.

After a pause, Elizabeth said, more collectedly, "Mr. MacLennan was just telling me about the people he works with."

"Oh yes?" David looked at Euan enquiringly.

"I was telling Lady Kinnell about Mr. and Mrs. Gilmour, the owners of *Flint's*," Euan said, a hint of defiance in his tone, as though he thought David wouldn't approve. "I was explaining that it was Mr. Gilmour who founded the paper, but Mrs. Gilmour is just as involved. As we all are. It is a collective endeavour. We all have a say-so in what happens."

He glanced at Elizabeth. "I wish you could meet them," he said. "They are a most unusual couple."

Elizabeth tilted her head to the side. "Oh? Why is that?"

"They live as equal partners," Euan said. "They drew up an agreement before their marriage that whatever the law might say, Mrs. Gilmour's property was to remain her own, that her rights over their children would be equal to her husband's, and that she owed him no obligation to obey his commands."

Elizabeth was silent for a moment; then she said, sounding bewildered, "Why would they do that?"

"They believe that Woman should not be Man's

slave," Euan said simply. "And if I ever marry, I will do just as they have done. If I marry, I don't want a domestic slave."

"No?"

"No. Man's oppression of Woman is the first, and worst, act of oppression in human history. Until we repair that, how can we repair the other inequalities all around us? Every child grows up witnessing this most grievous form of slavery. We drink it in with our mothers' milk and take it for the natural order. But it is *not*."

Elizabeth swallowed, as though past a lump, her pale throat working almost painfully. She looked away, averting her face.

"You are passionate about this," David observed into the silence that followed. It occurred to him that if he was being a proper host, he would change a subject that seemed to be causing one of his guests distress, but he couldn't help thinking that it may do Elizabeth good to hear this.

Euan turned his head to look at David. "I am," he admitted. "My father beat my mother like a dog. One night, it was so bad Peter took a poker to him and drove him out of the house. He never came back. Peter was only fourteen, and the rest of us all under ten. Mam died a few days later. He'd broken something inside her, and we couldn't afford a physician."

Elizabeth made a choked sound at that, and Euan

turned to her at once, paling at her look of distress.

"I'm so sorry," he said. "I forgot myself—I shouldn't have spoken so frankly."

"No, no," she said, shaking her head. "It's just that—it's horrible, Mr. MacLennan. Losing your mother in such an awful way. My own father is such a *gentle* man, isn't he, Mr. Lauriston?"

David nodded. "Your father is the very best of men," he agreed, noticing she made no mention of her husband.

"Why can't all men be like that?" she asked, and though the question was put quietly, somehow David knew it was a cry from the heart. Those expressive eyes, wounded and astonished, gave her away.

David watched her carefully. "I don't understand it," he said. "There were at least two women in my home village who were regularly beaten by their husbands. One of them was a cousin of my mother's. She used to take refuge in our home when her man had been drinking. It's worst for women like that, who are poor. They have no power to change their circumstances. No financial power—"

"*No* woman has any financial power!" Elizabeth interrupted raggedly.

David fell silent.

"No married woman," she added, shambling her neutral mask back on.

"You're right, of course," David agreed evenly,

watching her. The swift rise and fall of her chest betrayed her extreme agitation. "Even a rich woman is a pauper in marriage."

"It's not merely that married women *have* no property, Mr. Lauriston," Elizabeth replied quietly. "It's that they *are* property."

"Mrs. Gilmour says that marriage is a form of slavery, under the law," Euan said then. "It is the greatest of all injustices."

Elizabeth nodded, then flushed, as though she'd only just realised what she'd given away. She averted her gaze and shrugged one slender shoulder. "I suppose it could be like slavery, if the husband wields his power unfairly." She gave a false little laugh. "Goodness, how serious we are being, and on such a day! Do you think the procession will come back down the hill soon? I am going to have a look."

Just like that, she broke away from the two men and hastened across the room to the window where her sister stood. Putting an arm around the other woman's waist, she tilted her head to rest on Catherine's shoulder.

"I'll warrant she knows precisely what it is to submit to the yoke of marriage," Euan muttered when she was out of earshot. "Did you see her neck, Davy?"

David nodded. "Looked like fingerprints." He paused, then added, even more quietly, "I've heard some things about her husband."

"What things?"

"Not much. Just that he brutalised younger boys at school."

"Once a brute, always a brute," Euan muttered. "She should leave him."

"He is her husband—if she ran away from him, he would be within his rights to demand she return." David swallowed against the sick feeling that observation stirred in him. "He owns her."

Euan didn't say anything to that, but he pressed his lips together, his eyes still fixed on the two sisters.

"I really did remember her, you know," he said at last. "From that assembly we went to. She waved at you. Then later, you danced with her. She looked at you like you'd hung the moon in the sky for her. I was sure she was in love with you."

"She wasn't in love with me," David murmured. "She was just being a typical young lady at an assembly. Happy. Excited."

"I know what I saw." Euan turned his head and smiled at David. "I thought you were a lucky dog. Did you make a bid for her hand? I suppose her family thought you weren't good enough?"

David shook his head. "I didn't think of her in that way, but even if I had, her mother would have opposed me, I imagine."

He didn't mention that Chalmers would have given him his eldest daughter's hand in a heartbeat.

"Can you imagine what they would think of someone like me?" Euan laughed, though his laughter held a bitter tinge. "A working-class radical without so much as two brass ha'pennies to rub together. Yet I would make a better husband than the one she has, if those bruises are anything to go by."

They stood for a moment longer, united in silent agreement. Then the wheezing drone of the bagpipes started up outside and Catherine gave a squeal of excitement and everyone rushed to the windows again to watch the procession come back down the Lawnmarket from Castlehill.

Euan took a notebook and a bit of worn-down pencil from the inside pocket of his coat. He began to make quick, neat notes in his book. David saw the pages were close-written, the lines economically crossed, written right to left, then bottom to top, the results almost indecipherable.

Euan glanced at David, noting his interest. "I was telling the truth, you know," he muttered. "I *am* a journalist."

"And is that the only reason you came to Edinburgh? To write a story?"

"Yes."

Just that. *Yes.*

There were so many other questions David wanted to ask. Had Euan searched for Hugh Swinburne when he ran away two years ago? Was that what had taken him to London in the first place? And if he was only here as a journalist, why come to see David? That last one bothered him enough that he put it to Euan, keeping his voice low.

"Did you really come to my door today looking for a view?"

A pause. "No, of course not."

Ah.

"What then?"

Euan reached into his coat again. "I wanted to give you this." He drew out a small leather purse, which he pressed into David's hand.

"What's this?"

It was a stupid question. He could see very well what it was, and feel the weight of the coins inside.

"It's the money you gave me," Euan said. "I told you I'd repay you, didn't I?"

David frowned, remembering Euan's serious gaze as they parted on an empty stairwell of the Imperial Hotel, remembering pushing his purse into Euan's hands and urging him to get away.

Not to look back.

"Thank you," David murmured. He didn't know what else to say. He'd never looked to get the money back and he didn't need it. But clearly it was important to Euan that the debt be repaid, so he tucked the purse into his pocket.

"How long will you be in town?" he asked after a

pause.

"For the duration of the King's stay. I'll write three or four pieces, I expect. *Impressions of Edinburgh During the King's Visit*. Something like that." Euan nodded at the window. "It won't all be about this type of thing. Tomorrow I'm going down to the Cowgate slums."

"I wouldn't have thought you'd need to visit them to write about them," David replied quietly. "You've stayed there yourself."

"That feels like a long time ago," Euan replied.

"Only two years."

"A lot's changed for me since then. Unpopular as *Flint's* is with the powers that be, it sells well and I get paid good money for what I do. I live quite well now. Not as grand as you"—he smiled, raising an eyebrow at David—"but well enough. I've gotten used to my comforts. I need to go back to remind myself what it's like in those old tenements."

Just then, the rest of David's guests sent up a little cheer, drawing their attention back to the windows. Euan craned his neck to see out and began to scribble in his notebook again.

It wasn't long before the procession was over, the cavalcade of peers and troops on its way down the Mound, the crowds that had lined the streets below since early morning slowly dissipating.

Within half an hour of it being over, a knock came

at the door. David went to answer it and was surprised to find a footman in livery standing there. His thin, pale face was coolly impassive but for the faintest curl of his upper lip. That curl—that almost imperceptible sneer—betrayed his contempt of David's modest rooms.

"Lady Kinnell's manservant," the man said by way of clipped introduction. "Here to escort her to her carriage."

Suddenly, Elizabeth was at David's shoulder.

"Fraser," she said in a strained tone of voice. "What are you doing here? Mr. Ferguson is taking me home."

Fraser's expression didn't alter. "His lordship sent me," he informed her. The tone of his voice was neutral, and yet that faint sneer remained in place.

David could see that this man did not respect his mistress.

Elizabeth nodded jerkily. "I need to put my bonnet on," she said. "Wait here, please."

David didn't like the way the man inclined his head, as though granting her leave. He didn't like his cold demeanour or his watchfulness. He had the distinct feeling that every detail Fraser saw was being stored away for future use.

When Elizabeth came back, she had her sister and brother-in-law in tow. Catherine looked as though she was trying to hide her anger. Ferguson looked wary.

"It's perfectly all right," Elizabeth was saying to her

sister soothingly. "Alasdair's just being considerate. He's very protective; you know that."

Catherine looked far from convinced. Her brow was pleated with worry, her normally smiling mouth pinched and unhappy. Her frown didn't ease even when Elizabeth leaned in to buss her cheek.

"Will we see you tomorrow, Lizzie?" she asked, a fretful edge to her voice.

"I hope so," said Elizabeth with a small smile, one that she extended to her sister's husband before she turned to David. Her expression became very reserved.

"Thank you for your hospitality, Mr. Lauriston," she said coolly. Her tone invited no intimacy in front of her watchful manservant.

"You're welcome, my lady," David said, equally formally, taking his lead from her. He thought he saw a glimmer of gratitude in her dark gaze for a moment, but it was gone so quickly he might've imagined it, and then she was sweeping out the door, her servant at her heels.

It struck David as he watched her leave that she looked as though she was going to face some ordeal, and that the man escorting her acted more like a gaoler than a manservant.

Was he being fanciful? Reading more into what he saw because of what Balfour had told him? But no, Elizabeth's own words, her distress at Euan's story about his mother, the way she hid herself behind that distant mask in front of her servant, and most of all, those bruises on her neck—all of it pointed to something being terribly wrong. As David closed the door behind her, he couldn't help but feel worried and angry. Couldn't help but wonder if he would ever see her again, or if her husband would spirit her off to his estate, far away in Galloway, and keep her there.

"Davy."

He turned to find Euan standing behind him, seeming agitated. The Fergusons must've returned to the parlour—there was no one else in the hall.

"I'm sorry, but I must go now," Euan said. His eyes flickered past David to the closed door. "I had no idea what time it was. I'm...a bit late for something."

He stepped forward, and David automatically moved aside.

"You'd better away, then," David said, adding truthfully, "It was good to see you, Euan."

Euan stopped midstep, caught in the doorway. He turned to David, his gaze oddly intent, as though he was considering saying something. In that moment, he seemed more like the old Euan than he had at any other time today, fresh-faced and youthful, his fair hair falling down over his brow, his sandy lashes doing nothing to veil his searching gaze. A handsome man, this one—and a serious one. "It was good to see you too," he said. A pause. "I didn't just come to return the money, you know."

"No?"

"No. I wanted to thank you for everything you did for me."

"I didn't do anything."

"Yes, you did. You helped me over and over again—and you stopped me making the biggest mistake of my life. I'll always be grateful to you."

For a moment, he looked as though he'd say more, but the only other words that came out were a mumbled, "Good-bye, Davy," and then he was out the door and heading down the stairwell at a run, his boots clattering on the stone steps.

Chapter Five

Friday, 16th August, 1822

Chalmers was not well. He didn't seem as bad as he'd been in the spring, but he looked worryingly tired. Shrunken too, his once-round frame swamped by a brocade dressing gown that would have fit him snugly when David first met him. Pain etched deep grooves into his forehead and at either side of his mouth.

"Thank you for coming round," the older man said, smiling weakly. "As you can see, I'm under the weather again." They were sitting in his study, Chalmers ensconced in the large chair behind the desk, David on the other side. It was their usual sitting arrangement and would have felt quite ordinary, had Chalmers been dressed for business. In his dressing gown, though, he looked incongruous.

"It's no trouble." David smiled, disguising his worry behind an easy expression.

"I wanted to ask you a favour," Chalmers continued. "I'm supposed to be part of the faculty's delegation at Holyrood on Monday, but there's no question of me being able to go. Will you go in my place?"

The faculty's opportunity to meet with and address the King? Was Chalmers serious?

David laughed, shaking his head. "Me? There must be fifty men who'd be more suitable to replace you. More eager too."

Chalmers's expression didn't alter. He was utterly unreadable when he wanted to be. "I've already spoken to the Dean, and he's agreed."

David frowned then. After a pause, he said, "Why do you want this? What's it really about?"

Chalmers smiled as though amused by David's suspicion. "What am I always telling you, lad? You need to move in the right circles, talk to the right sort of people. Call it leading the horse to water, if you like."

David's heart sank. "Is that it? You don't have to—"

"Oh, I think I do. You keep burying yourself in your books and hoping people will appreciate you for your work. The trouble is they don't."

"You do."

"I won't be around forever."

David swallowed, wondering how serious Chalmers's illness was. "I don't want to let you down," he said after a brief silence.

Chalmers gave a soft, wheezy chuckle. "You won't.

In fact, you *can't*, not when I don't really care what happens once you get there. The fact is, I'm not obliged to find a replacement, but I told the Dean I wanted to so I could send you.

"I know you hate the thought of going, but please, consider it. The other five delegates are the Dean, the Vice-Dean, Braeburn, MacIver and Irvine. It's an excellent opportunity to further your acquaintance with them. Apart from MacIver, they all have more work than they can manage."

David sighed. "How can I say no when you've gone to such trouble?"

"That's the spirit." Despite his hearty words, Chalmers's voice was thready, and his skin had a greyish hue. He closed his eyes, as though their conversation had tired him.

"Are you well?" David asked, placing his hand on the older man's where it rested on the desk. "Should I call for a servant?"

Chalmers shook his head. "I'll be all right in a minute. Stay. I wanted to talk to you about something else."

"All right." David sat back and waited for Chalmers to rally a bit. There was a tightness about the man's jaw, as though he was in pain. Eventually, though, his grim expression relaxed a bit, and he seemed to come back to himself.

"Elizabeth is in town," he said at last. "I gather

from Catherine that you've seen her?"

David nodded. "They came to watch the procession from my rooms."

"How did she seem to you?"

David paused, considering how to respond. He didn't want to worry the older man, but…

"She didn't seem her usual self," he said at last, honestly.

Chalmers's face seemed to crumble a little, as though David's words were both a worry and a relief. "I'm anxious about her," the older man admitted. "She's been different since her marriage. Subdued. Lizzie was never subdued with me."

Not with anyone, David thought, but he stayed silent, waiting for Chalmers to reveal the purpose of this shared confidence.

"I never wanted that marriage," Chalmers continued after a while, his usual calm demeanour fracturing to reveal the concerned parent. "I thought she'd choose someone—well, never mind what I thought. I'm just worried. She doesn't seem *happy*."

His anxious gaze landed on David, and in that moment, David understood that his own fears had not been idle. Her own father had seen the same changes in her and reached the same conclusions.

"What do you need from me?" he asked quietly.

Chalmers sighed. "If something happens to me, I don't want her to have no one she can go to. I don't want her to be isolated. Her mother—" He broke off, taking a deep breath before continuing more calmly. "I'd feel better if I knew someone else was keeping an eye on her. I know it's a lot to ask, but I don't know who else to speak to. Donald's a good lad, but he's not the type to make waves."

It *was* a lot to ask. Elizabeth lived in London, and her husband was a wealthy peer, capable of destroying David's career if he got on the man's wrong side. What Chalmers was asking of him could cost him very dear.

He wouldn't need to say no to sidestep the responsibility that Chalmers was seeking to give him. It would be easy to give a few meaningless reassurances that he'd do what he could, while pointing out the practical difficulties. But David couldn't do that. Had never been able to walk away from a cry for help.

"I'll watch out for her," he said, meeting Chalmers's troubled gaze with his own certain one. "And should she need it, I'll do everything I can to help her. I promise you."

David took his leave of Chalmers after a light dinner. It was dark when he left—yet not. Up the hill, on Queen Street, a faint haze of light glowed above the roofs of the townhouses. At first it puzzled him, but by the time he'd strolled halfway up the hill, he could hear the babble of the accompanying festivities. It was, he realised, the sound and reflected brilliance of the Illuminations, a grand spectacle that had been arranged in celebration of the King's arrival.

The royal yacht had finally arrived at the harbour of Leith two days ago, but aside from taking part in his official welcome at Leith yesterday—and the inevitable procession that followed—the King had not been seen. It seemed, however, that the people's disappointment at the King's evident lack of enthusiasm was being effectively diverted by the sights that greeted David when he reached Queen Street and beheld the city...

...aglow.

Everywhere, there was light.

David had heard about the plans for the Illuminations—they had been much discussed—but nothing could have prepared him for the magnificence of them. Queen Street teemed with people gawking at the wonders around them, and David joined them, merging into the vast crowd. The facades of the public and commercial buildings were festooned with flowing fabrics and cleverly cut paper transparencies, all of them vivid and glowing with light. There were images of the King, Britannia, saltires, thistles and lions rampant, every kind of patriotic flummery, lighting up the dark and shivering in the breeze. It was amazing. Spectacular and unprecedented. Who would have thought this grey, sober city had in it so much colour?

A sudden explosion made David jump, then laugh as a shower of red and gold embers lit the sky. Another rocket went off, and another, one after the other like an artillery of guns. The explosions of light seemed somehow disconnected from the sounds, spontaneous fire bursts appearing out of nowhere, brief and amazing, leaving nothing behind but a drift of smoke that hung in the sky with nowhere to go.

The spectators—David among them—laughed and gasped and cried out at the wonder of the display, letting out a collective sigh of disappointment when the rockets finally stopped.

It was strange, he thought as he walked on, that such a simple thing had lightened his heart so much. What had he witnessed but a few coloured lights? The brief fellow-feeling of that shared laughter and joy. Yet he felt happier than he remembered feeling in ages, and more alive. Excited too, though he wouldn't let himself think about the reason for that.

"You know where my house is."

He allowed himself to be carried along with the crowd as he gazed at the wonders around him. He was drawing closer to a house he'd visited once before, but it wasn't his doing. The crowd was taking him there. He just allowed it to happen.

"Come anytime..."

The local householders had become involved in the Illuminations too, it seemed. Every window on the street blazed with candles, the drapes thrown open, some of their occupants staring out at the street below. The light from all those windows brightened the streets till it was almost like daytime, or at least that part of the day before darkness truly falls. High above them, on the other side of Princes Street Gardens, the castle glowed too, its battlements strung with a necklace of fiery braziers.

David drifted along, stopping briefly to chuckle with the other bystanders at a group of four sailors dancing a drunken hornpipe while a fifth tootled on a reedy flute.

A battery of guns started thundering from the east. The guns on the Calton Hill, David guessed. More salvoes pounded out from the castle's guns to the south, and a scattering of cheers went up.

"God save the King!" someone called out, a sentiment that was echoed over and over again.

When the guns stopped, the crowd began to move again, carrying David farther east. For a while, he strolled along Queen Street with everyone else, till he realised where he was. Standing at last in front of that house he remembered so very well.

The crowd behind him pressed at him, but he resisted its friendly push. Instead, he stood there and let people flow around him, like water round a river boulder, as he stared at a familiar door with dark, glossy paintwork and a gleaming brass knocker.

"You know where my house is."

He'd entered this house for the first time two years ago, and what happened here had been a defining moment in his life. He had given up something of himself in this place, and the experience had changed him in some way he still found difficult to put into words.

Even now he could remember every detail of that night: lying in a bed with another man for the first time, the flickering patterns made by the candlelight on the ceiling while his partner's mouth pleasured him. His partner—Murdo Balfour. Balfour leaning over him, taking his own pleasure, his dark gaze hot and possessive.

David sagged against the iron railings in front of Balfour's house and looked up at the windows above him, his chest aching. As with all the other private houses on the street, the drapes were open, the windows illuminated. And two floors up, a solitary figure stood at the drawing room window, staring out.

It was as though a giant hand gripped David, crushing him till he couldn't breathe. He stared, his hungry gaze eating up the picture Balfour presented, alone in his elegant castle.

Why should that sight make David feel so sad?

Why should it make him feel anything at all?

Just then, Balfour shifted. He began to scan the crowd on the street below his house, as though he'd felt David's attention somehow, like a physical touch. Or heard it, a silent call.

David watched, waiting helplessly for Balfour to

find him, and moments later, he did. His wandering gaze halted on David, and their gazes caught and held—for an instant, no more—before Balfour whirled away from the window and was gone.

It occurred to David, somewhere in the back of his mind, that now might be a wise time to leave; that further encounters with Murdo Balfour might not be prudent. But he didn't move. He leaned against the railings and stared at the glossy front door. And half a minute later, when it swung open, sure enough, there was Balfour, limned in light, a bright, excited smile on his handsome face. "Mr. Lauriston," he called, lifting his voice against the chatter of the crowd and beckoning with his arm. "Won't you come in?"

David found himself walking towards the short flight of steps that led to Balfour's open door. He moved like a man in a dream, travelling west against a river of people flowing east, and ascended the steps. When he finally halted in front of Balfour, he had not the slightest idea of what to say, only hesitated, greedily taking in the picture the other man presented. Balfour's habitual expression of faintly mocking amusement—one lifted brow, a curl to his lip—seemed to have deserted him, and an unfamiliar tenderness warmed his dark gaze.

"It's good to see you again," Balfour said. "I was afraid...we wouldn't get another chance."

David frowned at that comment, and for some

reason that provoked a smile from Balfour. The lines at the corners of his eyes deepened with gentle merriment.

"Come in," he repeated, this time putting his hand round David's shoulder and propelling him forward. "Come and take a glass of wine with me at least."

Perhaps it was the dreamlike quality of the evening that made David accept Balfour's invitation. The night seemed filled with infinite possibility. Infinite magic. He murmured his agreement and followed Balfour inside and up a set of stairs that felt familiar enough to imbue him with an unsettling sense of déjà vu as he mounted them. At the top of the stairs, they turned to walk down a corridor that led to a cavernous set of rooms he remembered all too well.

No open drapes here. No, this was very private indeed.

"Wine?" Balfour offered, crossing the room to a sideboard that already held a half-drunk glass of burgundy liquid.

"Yes, please."

Balfour topped up the glass he'd been drinking from and poured another, handing the fresh one to David. Again that feeling of déjà vu spiked, drenching David in memories of standing in this very room, drinking Murdo's wine and wondering what he'd been thinking of to come here. Wondering what the night would bring.

He took a healthy swallow from his glass, hoping to calm the nerves clamouring in his gut.

Balfour said, "I'd just been thinking of you. I couldn't believe it when I looked out my window, and there you were, looking up at me."

"I didn't plan to come. I was caught up in the Illuminations and came upon your house unexpectedly." David felt a flush stain his cheeks at the half lie.

The quirk of Balfour's lips was oddly tender. "I suppose it was too much hope that you couldn't stay away." He paused, then added, "But I'm glad Fate brought you here." He raised his glass in brief salute, then drank deeply, and, after a moment, David followed suit. Somehow they both ended up draining their glasses.

David's glass dangled from his fingertips, the wine warming his blood. He couldn't think what to say, what to do, just stared at Balfour, tall and elegant in his expensive coat and pristine linen, as perfectly put together as a man could be. A knot of yearning twisted inside him, a yearning that was all tied up with his memories and with the way Balfour studied him, his gaze suddenly gone hot with desire.

Balfour crossed the space between them and tugged the cool glass from David's fingers, setting it aside and taking David's face in his hands, bringing their lips together—

—in a kiss.

For an instant, David froze, passive and disbelieving, as Balfour's lips pressed against his own; then he groaned, lifting his hands and fisting them in Balfour's clothes, gripping him, and pulling him closer with jerky, desperate movements. Balfour reciprocated, and then they were half embracing, half grappling, mouths opening and tongues tangling, both of them gasping for air between rough, wet kisses.

It had been two years. It felt like forever, and it felt like no time at all.

"I need—" Balfour muttered between kisses. "Need to see you."

They worked together, undoing buttons and buckles and knots, unpeeling coats and waistcoats and neck cloths, till they were both down to their breeches. And Christ but the heat and silk of Balfour's skin rubbing against his own made David half-mad with lust.

"Let me suck you," Balfour muttered, dropping to his knees, his hands going to the placket of David's breeches, his lips pressing against David's fabric-covered crotch as he worked the buttons free with nimble fingers. He drew David's cock out and engulfed the firm flesh in his hot, wet mouth.

David cried out, his fingers tunnelling into Balfour's dark hair, his hips helplessly bucking forward. God, the man's mouth was heavenly.

"Balfour—" he moaned.

At the sound of his own name, Balfour pulled his

mouth off David's cock and leaned back on his heels. David looked down, blinking, to meet a sloe-black gaze that was half-pleading and half-angry.

"My name is *Murdo*."

"Murdo," David repeated dazedly, the sound of it unfamiliar to him, intimate.

Balfour—Murdo—dipped his head again, and the heat and silk of his mouth enveloped David's cock again. Oh, the luscious pull of those lips. The sinuous twining of that tongue. And—yes, there—the sudden astonishing space as Murdo opened his throat and let David slide all the way back.

"I'm not going to last—" David gasped.

Murdo's only answer was to grip David's hips harder, applying his mouth more eagerly to the task, and in moments, David climaxed straight down his throat in a crisis more intense that any he could remember. As though Murdo had drawn something more than mere seed from him.

As soon as he finished, he felt ashamed of his eagerness. He'd lasted a minute at most, perhaps not even that. He'd never climaxed so quickly before, and he felt his cheeks suffuse with colour again. When he looked down at Murdo, it was to encounter a self-satisfied grin.

"Good lord, how long has it been for you?" the man teased as he raised himself to his feet.

"A while," David mumbled. "Sorry." He stepped

forward and reached for the placket of Murdo's own breeches to return the favour.

Before he could loosen a single button, Murdo's hand was on his, stopping him.

"I want this to last," he said, smiling, the little creases at the corners of his eyes ridiculously appealing. "Kiss me again."

David had been reluctant to kiss this man when they'd first met, but now, tonight, he didn't hesitate. Maybe it was the magic of the night again, or maybe the words themselves, spoken like an incantation, Murdo's softer, English-sounding accent caressing the syllables slowly. Whatever it was, David obeyed him, his hand snaking up to curl round the other man's neck, drawing him down so that their lips could meet again.

The taste of his own seed was in Murdo's mouth. The salty brine of life. Salt on his tongue, and the taste of Murdo too. The scent of him, in David's nostrils as they kissed deeper still.

Ah, this was madness. He should stop this now and go. Pleasure was all very well, but when it was like this, when his senses were tricked into thinking this could be more than the mere scratching of an itch, there were consequences. Bittersweet regrets. Memories that were all the harder to bear for their remembered pleasure. Life was easier sometimes when you didn't know what you were missing.

But already it was too late to stop. He'd started a brand-new memory, and even now, knowing what it would be like to lie in his lonely bed weeks from now and remember this, the wanting, the craving was stronger. He could no more walk away from this than a starving man could refuse bread.

And what pleasure. These kisses. The intimacy of them. The rough of Murdo's chin scraping his own, the give of his lips. His tongue, teasing the corner of David's mouth and the *feel* of his smile—lips curving up against David's. David opened his eyes at that smile, just in time to see Murdo's own lashes flutter open. And, the shock, the shock and the pleasure of meeting a gaze that expressed so perfectly what David felt at this moment: wonder, pleasure...unexpected affection.

Murdo broke the kiss first, though he curled his fingers round David's jaw, keeping him in place and brushing David's damp lips with the warm, fleshy pad of his thumb.

"Come to bed," he husked.

He drew David—heart thudding, breath still coming fast from their kisses—into the neighbouring bedchamber, halting at the end of the bed. He knelt, divesting David of his remaining, already loose clothing before unfastening and removing his own. When he stood again, fully naked, he pulled David flush against him.

"You're different than last time," he murmured. "More...amenable."

"Am I? I feel just as overwhelmed."

"Overwhelmed?" Murdo's gaze was teasing and curious at once.

David hated the blush that returned to heat his cheeks yet again. His ready blush was the one thing he could never control, a horribly obvious betrayal of his feelings. "I'd never done this with anyone else before you," he admitted.

Murdo frowned. "Of course you had. You knew what you were abou—"

"Like this, I mean," David interrupted tightly. "In a bed."

"Oh." Comprehension transformed Murdo's expression. He turned David round and gently pushed him down onto the mattress till he lay flat on his back, then settled himself at David's side, his hand propping up his head. It was all David could do not to grab hold of him. Despite having only just climaxed, David's cock was as hard as stone all over again, aching with need. How Balfour could lie there, just studying David's prone body with calculated patience, was beyond him.

When Murdo finally touched him, it was to smooth his hair back from his forehead.

"Last time we did this, you told me you'd didn't allow anyone to fuck you," he said, watching David carefully.

"I still don't."

"You won't let me do that, then?"

David paused. The truth was, he'd thought about that very possibility a great deal over the last two years. And about what it meant to lie with another man; what it was that made a man a *sodomite*. About the thoughts he had that made him hard and needy in the dark hours of the night, and the images that floated into his mind while he serviced—or was serviced by—another faceless man. It certainly wasn't the case that he had no desire to be fucked. But it was still something that petrified him, though perhaps in a different way than it used to.

Slowly, almost reluctantly, David shook his head.

"All right. How about we pleasure each other at the same time?"

David's mind raced, considering possibilities.

"Lie on your side," Murdo murmured, and David obeyed, shifting his body into position while Murdo turned his own around. When he was done, they lay head to crotch, their bodies mirroring each other. Then, without giving David time to think, Balfour engulfed David's prick in his mouth.

It shouldn't have been a surprise in the circumstances, but having already climaxed, it felt oddly rude and astonishing. Paralysed by pleasure, it wasn't till Murdo's cock stabbed at his chin that David woke up enough to play his own part in the mutual pleasuring Murdo had initiated. The blunt, reddened tip of Murdo's prick bobbed for attention, butting at David's lips, the skin impossibly soft. David inhaled, and Murdo's musky scent teased at him, heady and good.

Rather than swallow him straight down, David rubbed his cheek against Murdo's shaft and burrowed his nose into the thatch of dark hair at his groin before pressing his lips against the hot flesh. He lapped at it with the flat of his tongue, adoring, moving up the length of it before sucking it into his mouth.

He felt Murdo's reaction in the vibration of the other man's throat around his own cock as Murdo groaned his pleasure, and just like that, David's attention was diverted—he had to make a conscious effort to force himself to continue to attend to the other man, even though that was a pleasure too. The whole business was like that—a dizzying push-and-pull between giving and receiving, acting and reacting.

David caressed Murdo's scrotum with his fingertips while taking him right to the back of his throat, relishing even the choking sensation that brought—at least it kept his attention on Murdo's prick, a desperate challenge when the other man's mouth was doing such wicked things to his own. God, but this mutual pleasuring had him wildly distracted—hot, sucking wetness round his prick, and hard, silky flesh in his mouth, sensation everywhere, cock, mouth, lips, balls, almost too much, too good.

After a few minutes of this insane bliss, Murdo's fingers dug into David's hips, and he groaned again, his own mouth going slack and inattentive round David's prick. At the same time, his cock thickened in David's mouth and his hips began to jerk, searching for the back of David's throat. He was going to come, David realised, and the thought heightened his own urgent pleasure. He took hold of Murdo firmly, one hand on his buttock, the other gripping his pistoning hip, controlling the movement as he gave himself over to an abandoned frenzy of sucking.

A moment later, Murdo was crying out his pleasure, his seed exploding into David's mouth like a wash of sea water.

"Christ, David!" Murdo gasped. "What you do to me—"

And then his head was burrowing back into David's lap, his mouth working David's aching shaft for the second time. And despite that first endless, wrenching crisis, David was coming all over again, his body bowing as Murdo Balfour turned him inside out.

Chapter Six

When David woke up, Murdo had rolled away to the other side of the bed and a grey, tentative dawn was poking through the drapes, reminding him of the world outside.

He propped himself up on one elbow and watched as Murdo—or was he Balfour again this morning?—slept. He knew he should rise and dress but there was something fascinating about Murdo Balfour, even in repose. In sleep, the urbane mask entirely fell away. In sleep, his expression gentled, and the tender skin of his eyelids gave him a vulnerable look.

Murdo's temples were sprinkled with a few silver hairs. David wondered how old he was. He'd never said. He couldn't be more than six or seven years older than David, but he might be all of that. Perhaps two- or three-and-thirty. And unmarried still, it seemed. His dynastically minded father must find him a vexation.

He'd done his father's bidding in coming up for the King's visit, though. Playing the part of the Balfour clan chief's son for King and country. Had he felt silly, David wondered, parading up the High Street in with tartan paraphernalia? Murdo Balfour was the sort of man who usually dressed with severe, modern elegance—all dark superfine and snowy-white linen—David would never have thought he'd have put up with being dressed up like one of Walter Scott's fictional creations. Though it had to be said, he'd looked very well in dark-blue-and-green tartan.

Like Young Lochinvar.

He suppressed a smile at the thought. Unlike Young Lochinvar, Murdo was unlikely to be stealing anyone's bride.

Murdo.

Already David found it impossible to think of him as Balfour.

David glanced at the clock on the mantel. Half past six. Definitely time to leave. He shouldn't have stopped the night—the servants would be moving about the house soon, if they weren't already. The magic of the night was well and truly over.

For some strange reason, though, he felt no regret, no panic—not like last time, when his encounter with Balfour had sent him running off, out into the night, seeking some kind of oblivion. In fact, he felt more at peace than he normally did, as though all the jumbled parts of himself had been set right overnight.

What fanciful thoughts.

Sitting up, David extricated himself from the tangled bedcovers, moving carefully so as not to wake the other man. His efforts at silence were for nothing, though—the sounds of fabric brushing as he began to dress, along with the protests of the floorboards beneath his feet, were apparently enough to pull Balfour out of his dreams. The man stirred and opened his eyes just as David was buttoning up his breeches.

"You're leaving?" He yawned.

"I should go before one of your servants comes in."

Balfour sat up, rubbing a hand over his eyes. Boyishly rumpled, he was a different man from the elegant peer of last night—messier and altogether more human. And when he looked David up and down as he was doing now, the corner of his mouth kicking up in appreciation, he was so appealing he made David's mouth run dry.

"Don't worry about the servants," he said. "I brought some of my London staff with me. They're more discreet—they know never to enter my private rooms in the morning till I call for them. Besides"—he leaned back on his elbows and gave one of his half-hitch smiles—"it's Saturday. Spend the morning with me."

"Don't you have duties to perform?" David replied. His voice came out lower than he'd intended, rough with desire. He cleared his throat, adding, "I thought you were on the King's retinue."

"Not quite. I'm more one of the outer circle. As for today, I've no commitments other than the Levee this afternoon." He consulted the clock on the wall. "And it's not even seven. I've got a few hours before I go anywhere. Enough for a decent breakfast, at least. Join me."

"I should really—" David began automatically, then he broke off.

Why not just do as Balfour asked? Why not let himself enjoy the man's company for a few more hours? It was a pleasurable diversion from normal life, wasn't it? One that was safe from any fear of discovery and ruin, unlike his usual encounters. He'd already crossed the line by coming here, so why not enjoy the fruits of his recklessness to the full?

"All right," he said. "I'll stay a bit longer."

When Murdo grinned at him and flipped the bedcovers back, he felt a rush of joy that should have been alarming. But he didn't even let himself think about it. Instead he let himself have the moment, let the joy of it brighten him.

He stripped his breeches and drawers off again—the work of a moment—and impulsively leapt at Murdo, landing on top of him and knocking a surprised shout of laughter out of him. Murdo twisted, rolling David onto his back and under him, and they wrestled for a minute, muscles straining, bodies pressing and sliding, a brief tussle for dominance.

Bested, David stopped struggling, gasping with laughter, and Murdo stilled over him. Their gazes locked for the longest time, and David felt a queer ache in his chest. He had to close his eyes to gain control of himself.

When he opened them again, Murdo's gaze had shifted downwards. He laid his hand on David's chest, letting his fingertips drift over David's nipples, the flat planes of his chest, and the ridges of muscle below. His dark eyes were appreciative.

"You look slender in your clothes, but you're strong." He ran his hands up David's arms, testing the muscles there. "How do you manage it? Bookish fellows are usually softer."

"I walk a lot—I love to be outside, in the country. I like to climb too."

"Climb? What do you mean?"

David laughed, a little embarrassed. "Oh, you know. Hills, rock faces sometimes. Last month I climbed a bit of Salisbury Crags."

Murdo's eyebrows rose. "How very odd. Isn't that dangerous?"

"Well—yes."

Murdo laughed, delight sparkling in those pitch-dark eyes at David's artless response. "I'd love to see you climb. Perhaps you could take me, one day."

"Perhaps," David agreed, smiling, liking the thought of showing off to Murdo, for all the childish absurdity of it.

Murdo lowered his head, capturing David's lips with his own. His hand, caught between their bodies, coasted down David's chest, belly, flank. Those strong, determined fingers sought and found David's prick, rubbed it in long, luxurious strokes.

Grinding his hips, Murdo pushed his own cock forward, opening his grip so the blunt head pushed against David's, rude and insistent. Then his big hand was closing about both of them, pressing and rubbing them together, making David helplessly groan.

"You too," he breathed against David's mouth. "Put your hand over mine." David fumbled his hand down between them, his fingers interlacing with Murdo's to make a clumsy cage of flesh that began to move in exquisite, dragging counterpoint to the slide and grind of their shafts. Murdo's hips jerked against David's as they worked together, kissing as they went, nearly devouring each other. David was so beyond thought, he could do little more than let Murdo steer their joined hands while he lay, moaning incoherent encouragement, until they went over the edge together, their mingled seed spilling over their fingers and dripping onto David's belly.

They lay there together, sticky and sated, and David let his mind empty, let himself enjoy the languorous aftermath of orgasm.

"Do you remember that first time we were together

here, like this?" Murdo asked after a while.

David was staring up at the intricate petals of the ceiling rose. Murdo's voice in his ear was a surprise, but he didn't shift his gaze, just nodded. The truth was, he remembered that night as though it was yesterday; the impossible, unprecedented intimacy of it burned in his memory. Murdo's mouth on the entrance to David's body, his long fingers breaching, then moving inside David.

That night had undone him entirely. Changed him. There was no going back from something like that, something that had scuppered so many of his personal limits. Later, when Murdo was gone, returned to London, the memory of it had tormented him. Yet it had fortified him too somehow. Sometimes he hated that he'd done it, and other times, it felt like the only sane thing he'd ever done in all his life.

"I couldn't stop thinking about you after I went back to London," Murdo said roughly.

Astonished, David turned his head on the pillow to meet the other man's gaze. That face. So familiar, on such little acquaintance. As though he'd absorbed every detail about Murdo Balfour without realising it.

"Nor I you," he murmured before he could censor himself.

Murdo grew still. Watchful. "Really?"

The heat of an infuriating blush was on David's cheeks. "Yes, really."

"Why?"

Discomfited, David turned his head to look back up at the perfect plasterwork on the ceiling. "I don't know. I just—never knew it could be like that, between two men."

"Neither did I."

There was a long silence during which David tried hard not to swallow against the curious obstruction in his throat.

Then Murdo flung the covers aside and got out of bed. "Time for a bath," he announced briskly, reaching for the bell pull.

They ate breakfast at the small table in Murdo's private sitting room. Smoked haddock, eggs and potato cakes, a basket of warm, toasted muffins and a dish of fruit conserves. Everything served on fine, white porcelain dishes, with silver cutlery and white damask napkins. There was tea served in a silver teapot with milk and sugar presented in a matching silver jug and bowl. There were even tiny little silver tongs to pick up the sugar lumps.

David found he was unusually hungry. The food was excellent, the fish sweet and flaky, the eggs just done, with runny yolks that were heavenly spread on the potato cakes. He ate everything on his plate, then helped himself to a toasted muffin, spreading it thickly with cold butter that tasted almost as good as the stuff his mother made. He added a spoonful of crimson jam that gleamed like a pile of rubies and bit into the muffin with relish, catching Murdo's eye as he did so and noting his amused smile.

"What is it?" he said, after he'd swallowed the mouthful down. "Do I have something on my face?" He explored the side of his mouth with his fingertips.

"No, it's just that you're eating so…heartily."

David frowned. "So?"

Murdo shrugged, still smiling. "You never struck me as a man who enjoyed his food. In fact, I distinctly remember you telling me that sometimes you forget to eat."

"That doesn't mean I don't enjoy my food when I do eat," David retorted, but even as he spoke the words, it occurred to him that he couldn't remember the last time he'd enjoyed a meal as well as this one.

"Well, you must still forget too often. You're a bit on the thin side."

David's jaw tightened at the implied criticism. "You seemed to like the look of me well enough earlier."

"Oh, for God's sake." Murdo laughed. "You must know how much you appeal to me by now! You're as handsome as anyone could wish. There, will that do?"

David scowled, resenting the implication he'd been fishing for compliments and embarrassed by the one he'd been given. Uncomfortable with the turn in the conversation, he tried to steer it back to where it had begun. "I eat well enough," he muttered.

"You're a healthy enough specimen," Balfour agreed, leaning back in his chair and looking David over with an appreciative gaze. "But eating to live is one thing; eating for pleasure is quite another. You enjoyed that muffin. And I enjoyed watching you when you tasted it." He acted it out for David, biting into an imaginary muffin, his eyes closing with pleasure, lips curving upwards.

Reluctantly charmed by Murdo's playacting, David huffed out a laugh. "I didn't look like that."

Murdo opened his eyes again, quirking one dark brow. "Oh, you did. And it's how you were last night too. You surrendered to the pleasure. Was that the first time you've done that, David? It wasn't how you were the first time we were together."

That statement rocked David back on his heels. Over the past two years, whenever he had recalled his night with Murdo, his memory had been one of shocking, uncontrollable passion. Was it possible Murdo remembered it differently? Had he thought of David as inhibited? Reluctant?

"I think I showed how much I enjoyed myself that night—in the usual way," David replied, hating the defensive tone in his voice.

"You mean when you came for me?"

David squirmed, and Murdo smiled at his obvious embarrassment.

"I knew that you enjoyed it in the end," Murdo continued. "My point is that you didn't want to. You resisted it."

"I don't know why we're talking about this now," David said. He saw no point in this conversation, going over old ground that should be left well alone.

Murdo ignored that comment. "The last time you were in this house, part of you didn't want to be here at all. Part of you resisted everything we did together. I had to make you face up to what you wanted. Last night was different. *You* were different."

David met Murdo's dark gaze. Murdo was smiling in that bland, pleasant way he did sometimes that made him impossible to read. David wanted to tear that mask away and expose what was underneath, just as Murdo was exposing him.

"You were different last time too," he retorted.

Murdo's eyebrow rose. "Whatever do you mean?" There was amusement in his voice. The mask was still firmly in place.

"You pushed me," David said. "You did things to me you knew I'd never have permitted in my right mind."

He paused then, remembering. Considering, perhaps for the first time, what might have been going through Murdo's head that night. "I think you deliberately set out to provoke me," he said slowly. "Perhaps you wanted to see just how far you could push me."

Murdo's mask stayed in place, but the amusement had faded. After a long moment of silence, he said softly, "Is that what you think?"

David considered. "I think you enjoyed shocking me."

A flash in Murdo's dark eyes. He didn't like that.

"You make it sound like I was playing with you," he said.

"Weren't you?"

"No. I admit I wanted to shake you up—*wake* you up. But I just wanted you to see yourself!"

David gave a harsh laugh. "You assumed I didn't see myself already?"

"I *knew* you didn't," Murdo shot back. "Not as you are."

"That's where you're wrong. I already knew I preferred men. I'd known for—"

"You saw yourself as an abomination," Murdo interrupted flatly. "I wanted you to see you as I see you."

"And how exactly is that?"

"As someone—" Murdo broke off and looked away, nostrils flaring as he breathed out his anger. "You're not an abomination, David. You're—beautiful."

David's throat closed up for a moment, but he forced himself to speak, his voice thick with emotion.

"I'm a *man*, Murdo, not a woman to be courted."

"A man can't be beautiful?"

"I don't think—" David began, faltering when he remembered Murdo standing naked in the candlelight last night.

Beautiful.

"You still think this is wrong," Murdo accused, interrupting his wayward thoughts. "Even now, after what we shared last night. You think *you* are wrong." He stood abruptly, his chair scraping against the floor.

For a moment, he stared down at David; then he gave a huff of exasperation and turned away, crossing the room to stand before the window and look down at the gardens below.

You think you *are wrong.*

David racked his brains trying to find words to respond to that accusation. The truth was, he'd changed quite a lot since that first time with Murdo. In the months that had followed, he hadn't been able to get what had happened between them out of his mind. The memories had been both a torment and a comfort, nipping at him, agitating him, making him consider things he'd once have deemed unthinkable. The possibility of tenderness and affection. The possibility of honesty, of being *known* by another. Things he'd ruled out for himself. Things that were too painful to hope for.

Those memories had been something to cherish

too, a treasure he could take out and examine in his darkest moments. A remembrance that, for all his regrets, was rich with unexpected sweetness.

Slowly, David stood up from his own chair and crossed the room, coming to a halt behind the other man. Murdo had to hear his approach, but the only sign of awareness he gave was a slight tensing of his shoulders.

"I may not think I'm beautiful," David said at last. "But I don't think I'm precisely *wrong* either. Not anymore. Not since…you."

Murdo went very still. David felt like Murdo's whole body was listening to him.

"If I'm honest," David continued slowly, "I'm not sure *what* I think of myself now. But it's different to how I used to feel. Better, I mean."

Murdo turned slowly. "How did you used to feel?" A wary curiosity filled his gaze.

"Like I was—like I was damned to hell. Just for thinking about the sorts of things you and I did together last night." The words tumbled out of David in a torrent. He took a ragged breath, forcing himself to keep his eyes on Murdo.

"Don't you feel like that anymore?"

David shook his head, unable to say more.

Murdo gave a rough laugh. "It's not the *most* ringing endorsement I've ever received," he said.

"No?" David smiled weakly. "Well, you've no idea

how far I've come."

"Oh, I've an idea." Murdo raised a hand and touched David's jaw, an impossibly gentle brush of his fingers.

Time hung, silent, between them for a moment. Then Murdo said, like someone admitting an uncomfortable truth, "I'd like to see you again, while I'm here."

David stared into those intense, unsettling eyes. It was a bad idea. A terrible idea. He would pay if he gave in and let himself have this, because much as the last time had been a treasure, it had been a bittersweet one. There would be a price to pay for more memories like this. A black descent.

But there would be this too. This excited temporary joy. This pleasure.

When all was said and done, he couldn't bring himself to say no.

"I'd like that too," he murmured.

He was rewarded with a smile, an unguarded, happy one that made Murdo's dimple flash in his cheek. "When?"

"I don't know—aren't you going to be busy? With the King, I mean?"

Murdo sighed. "Quite a bit of the time, yes. Are you going to any of the events Sir Walter's organised?"

"Just to Holyrood on Monday, with some others from the faculty."

"Hmm. Is that when the good burghers of Edinburgh are to take turns at droning on about themselves while His Majesty smiles and nods?"

"The same," David agreed, a small smile twitching at his lips.

"I'll be there too. Can I see you after?"

David thought of how many people there would be at Holyrood. How chaotic it would be. How impossible.

How very unwise this was.

"Yes," he said. "Yes, I'd like that."

Chapter Seven

Monday, 19th August, 1822

David tweaked the saltire cockade on his hat and stood back to study his appearance in the small looking glass that sat on his dressing table, craning his neck this way and that.

It was the day of the ceremony at Holyrood, and he wore his new suit of clothes. He could only hope the Dean would find him up to scratch. The man had already made it clear that he considered David a very poor substitute for Patrick Chalmers.

It was going to be a long day. The King wouldn't arrive at Holyrood Palace till mid-afternoon but David and his fellow advocates were meeting at the Dean's house at eleven o'clock. The Dean's carriage would take them all to the palace, where the Dean and Vice-Dean had an early meeting with Sir Robert Peel. While they were thus engaged, the rest of their party would be dispatched to the Entrée Room to secure a good spot for the King's arrival. When the King arrived, the speeches would begin.

The thought of spending the day with some of the most senior men in the faculty should have pleased David, but in truth he dreaded the day ahead. The politics of the faculty—something that Chalmers seemed to negotiate with perfect ease—eluded him, even after six years, and he'd always felt the safest course of action was to steer well clear of it all.

Today, it would be unavoidable.

There was one thing that made it all bearable: Murdo Balfour would be there. Part of the King's entourage.

David hadn't set eyes on Murdo since that morning three days ago now. Already their time together felt unreal. The memory of their last conversation made David shake his head in bewilderment, even as it made him helplessly smile. Even as the rational part of him told himself to stop behaving like a besotted boy.

But really, what was the most that could happen between them? David might share Murdo's bed for another night or two, possibly even three. It would be a fleeting escape from the stuff of his ordinary life. A night or two to open himself up and let all his stored-up yearnings spill to the floor of Murdo Balfour's locked bedchamber.

But would his new memories be enough to sustain him against the realisation that it was over afterwards? The awful realisation that that was *it*.

Enough of that, David chided himself, frustrated at

the single-minded direction of his wayward thoughts. He had more immediate concerns. Time to be off. The Dean wouldn't tolerate lateness.

He walked briskly to the Dean's house, a beautifully appointed property on Charlotte Square. The day was overcast, but David thought they'd be spared rain. Not that it would matter, given that the rest of it would be spent cooped up indoors.

The door was answered by a maidservant in a neat cap and apron who showed David into the drawing room. Irvine and MacIver were already there. Both men were youthful as compared to the Dean but a good decade older than David.

"Hello, Lauriston," Irvine said, evidently surprised to see David. "What are you doing here?"

"Mr. Chalmers was prevented from attending by illness," David explained. "He asked me to come in his place."

MacIver snorted at that, but Irvine smiled and murmured, "Ah, new blood. Very good, very good. Come and sit with us."

They chatted about inconsequentialities while they waited, and, after a few minutes, the Dean joined them. He had the Vice-Dean with him, trotting at his heels like a faithful hound.

The Dean was a tall, thin man with a hook nose and a natural air of authority, whilst the Vice-Dean was his polar opposite. Rotund, amiable and somewhat vague, he'd always struck David as rather ineffectual.

"We're still waiting on Braeburn, I see," the Dean observed irritably. "I said ten o'clock, and it's almost half past the hour."

"The meeting with Peel isn't till twelve," the Vice-Dean observed in a soothing tone. "We have plenty of time."

"I like to be early," the Dean said in his usual clipped manner. "I like to get the lay of the land. This will be a tricky business."

"What's the meeting about?" MacIver growled. He was a perpetually bad-tempered man, communicating mainly in grunts and expletives. Why he'd been chosen as part of the delegation was beyond David's comprehension.

"Sir Robert is looking for more consistency in the criminal law, north and south of the border," the Vice-Dean explained. "He is meeting with the judges as well as ourselves, canvassing support for his ideas. You may be sure he is doing the same in Parliament."

MacIver scowled. "I don't like the sound of that. Our laws have long been different from those of the English. We have different histories, different principles."

The Vice-Dean smiled in his airy, benign way. "But does our different history really matter, MacIver," he asked, "if our objectives are the same?"

"Of course it does!" MacIver retorted. "Why should

we change centuries of Scots law at the whim of an English politician?"

"But what if we need new laws? To tackle those amongst us who would undermine the rule of law?"

He was alluding, of course, to the civil unrest that had plagued the whole of Britain over the last few years, on both sides of the border.

"Is that what Sir Robert wants to achieve?" David asked. "To make it easier to tackle radicals?" The other three men all turned to look at him, appearing as surprised as if a dog had spoken.

"I'm sure I don't know, but we may find out this afternoon," the Vice-Dean answered. His tone was as amiable as ever, though his gaze suddenly struck David as rather watchful.

Braeburn arrived then, the last of their number, apologising breathlessly. The Dean received his excuses coldly and called for the carriage. Within ten minutes, they were crammed inside the close confines of the Dean's old-fashioned brougham and were rumbling through the cobbled streets on their way to Holyrood Palace.

The Entrée Room at Holyrood Palace was horribly warm and growing ever warmer. For almost two hours, David had been standing, waiting. David and a few hundred others—the huge room fairly bristled with men, all of them awaiting the King's arrival. The few chairs in the room were at a premium and reserved for the more important—rather than the most needful—attendees.

The Dean and Vice-Dean had had their short audience with Sir Robert Peel, emerging tight-lipped about what had been said. The two of them sat on a pair of spindly chairs now, heads together, murmuring, while the rest of the faculty's delegation stood behind.

David wasn't troubled by the long wait, but some of the other gentlemen seemed really quite uncomfortable. Poor, portly Braeburn kept shifting from foot to foot and was now trying to surreptitiously rub one ample hip. His handkerchief must be soaked with sweat from the number of times he'd wiped his brow, and his face was red and shiny from the heat.

Braeburn wasn't the only one. All around, well-fed men in stiff, new clothes fidgeted and perspired in the stifling air. The delegation from the Kirk dominated the place. Over a hundred of them, and every one of them head-to-foot in Presbyterian black. Like a murder of crows, David thought. Or perhaps a parliament of rooks was more like it. Officious and proper. Committee-like.

The preponderance of black was broken up by the secular men in the room. Most of them, like David, wore Sir Walter's uniform of blue coat, light trousers and low-crowned hat, but a few wore highland clothes—red and green and purple tartans. These fellows stood out amongst their more sober neighbours like birds of paradise.

David knew the ceremony would be a long one. He'd heard the Kirk was to have its say first. Then the university men, the judges, the faculty, and finally, several groups of magistrates and burghers, both of Edinburgh itself and of a host of other surrounding towns and villages the King would never see. Address after address. It would go on for hours, each delegation taking its turn to pour out the same greetings, compliments and felicitations to the King who'd kept them waiting hours for the privilege.

Finally, at half past two, a great clattering in the courtyard outside heralded the arrival of the King's party. Men on horseback first, then the rumble of the wheels of coaches. At last, it seemed, the King was here.

The servants of the palace were being ordered around by an absurdly young-looking fellow who was apparently a junior member of the King's staff. His hairless cheeks shone pink with effort as he rushed to and fro, rapping out orders in a slightly high voice.

Earlier, the same young man had determined the arrangement of the occupants of the room according to some form of precedence known only to himself, offending several important personages in the process, the Dean among them. Now he was at it again, practically shoving the great and the good off their seats and exhorting the harried servants to remove the chairs from the room altogether so that everyone would have to stand in the King's presence.

The servants did his bidding, and a few minutes later, the doors to the Entrée Room were flung open, and the King entered, surrounded by an entourage of redcoats and well-dressed peers.

At first—and despite his size and the magnificence of his dress—David didn't notice the King. His gaze automatically sought Lord Murdo Balfour. He was easily found, with his height and striking dark looks, bringing up the rear of the royal party.

As the party moved farther into the room, David caught Murdo's eye. The man's lips twitched into an almost-smile as he drew closer, and David almost-smiled back, unable to stop the left corner of his mouth lifting. Murdo's dark eyes glinted with humour as he passed David to join the King in the centre of the room. At last, the ceremony began.

It was just as dull as David had feared. Worse even. The Kirk's address began with an obsequious welcome, but at length—great length—this turned into nothing short of a sermon, and a rather fire-and-brimstone one at that. If the King was perturbed by this, he didn't show, accepting what was said with a series of gracious but somewhat unfathomable nods.

The universities went next. They seemed to have resolved any issue over who should have the honour of addressing the King by splitting the job up amongst a bewildering number of professors, each of whom seemed determined to milk the opportunity for all it was worth. David felt his eyelids drooping several times and had to pinch himself awake.

At long last, it was the turn of the faculty, and finally David was moving his stiff limbs forward, following the Dean to stand before the King. They stood in a horizontal line, the six of them, even though only the Dean would be speaking.

It was David's first proper look at King George. A corpulent, high-coloured man, he wore the marks of longstanding self-indulgence in his heavy jowls and weak chin. His garments were generously cut, but still, he must be well-girdled beneath them to squeeze into his magnificent admiral's uniform of royal blue, braided with gold. Did he think himself truly a warrior to dress himself so, David wondered? So far as he knew, the man had never seen any kind of military service.

The King smiled at the faculty delegation benignly while one of his retinue murmured in his ear, explaining to him, no doubt, what the Faculty of Advocates was.

"Gentlemen," the King said when his adviser had pulled back. "It is a pleasure to meet with you."

They all bowed, somewhat awkwardly in David's case. As always in formal situations, he was conscious that his manners lacked polish, but he had no time to dwell on his deficiencies. The Dean was already stepping forward to speak.

"Your Majesty," the Dean said in the deep, sonorous voice he always used when giving an address. "The ancient and honourable Faculty of Advocates welcomes you, our beloved monarch, to Scotland, and thanks you, sincerely and humbly, for the privilege of addressing you."

The King smiled and inclined his head a little, and the Dean went on in much the same vein, delivering his carefully prepared speech in a slow cadence, seeming to relish every word.

David didn't dare look at Murdo. If Murdo looked amused, David would find it impossible to keep a sober expression on his own face. He was acutely aware of the man, though, standing just a few steps away.

Determinedly, he kept his attention on the King. It was surprising, David thought, that the King had decided to stand to hear the lengthy addresses, despite the warmth of the room and the staleness of the air.

The King was showing signs of growing discomfort. Initially, he had taken the sort of noble stance that might be assumed for a royal portrait: one foot pointed forward, his weight on the rear leg, his extended right arm holding a gold-topped cane that touched the floor but did not take any of the burden of his considerable bulk. It couldn't have been a comfortable pose, and he'd done well to hold it so long, but at this proximity,

David could see that his expression was growing strained, a beading of sweat breaking out over his heavyset face. His legs in his skintight breeches looked to be bloated, and every now again he shifted, resting a little more weight on the cane.

Had he realised quite how long he would end up standing? Surely someone would have warned him how lengthy this afternoon threatened to be.

David glanced at the Dean to see if he too had noticed the King's discomfort and if he intended to conclude his speech early. But the Dean seemed entirely oblivious. He was altogether caught up in his oratory, listing now the nations around the globe over which King George was sovereign and master, "A wise father to all his subjects."

What rot.

Given what he'd already noticed, David wasn't entirely surprised when, the instant he turned his attention back to the King, it was to see the man stumble, his cane clattering noisily to the floor. Without thinking, David dashed forward to steady him, offering his own rigid frame in support. For a brief moment, the King leaned on him, and David had to brace himself to bear the man's bulky weight even for that short time.

"Your Majesty," he gasped. "You should be sitting down. It is far too hot in here to be standing so long."

There were a few murmurings at that breach of

etiquette, but David ignored the shocked expressions, catching the eye of the high-voiced young man who had been ordering the removal of all the chairs earlier.

"Fetch a chair for His Majesty, if you please," David said loudly, abandoning any attempt at polite address.

The young man coloured with anger at David's command. He looked at the King, who was already rallying after his brief dizzy spell, pulling his weight back from David.

"Your Majesty—" the young man protested. Perhaps he was an aristocrat, offended to be dictated to by a commoner. Perhaps he thought the King should scold David for his rudeness.

"He's right, Sir Anthony," the King said snappishly. "It is…hot in here. So, do as he says and fetch me a chair, there's a good fellow."

Sir Anthony flushed an angry red, but he bowed deeply before stalking off to give the order to one of the palace staff.

The King was standing by himself again now, and David retreated back a step. He didn't yet return to his place, though, nervous the man might stumble again. Instead he waited for Sir Anthony's lackey to return with the chair. The delicate, spindly-legged thing he brought didn't look up to the job, particularly when the King dropped into the chair so heavily David thought the legs might give out. But it must have been stronger than it looked.

"What is your name, sir?" the King asked then, his gaze measuring David.

"David Lauriston, Your Majesty."

"And you are an advocate, like your friends?" He nodded at the Dean, who looked faintly offended to be bracketed with David as a "friend".

"I am, indeed."

The King smiled, benign and in control again, comfortable now in his new, seated position.

"Do you enjoy your profession, Mr. Lauriston?"

"I do, Your Majesty," David answered honestly.

The King smiled and nodded at him genially. "Very good," he said. It was a dismissal. David bowed and returned to his place.

The King cast a look over his shoulder, summoning someone. The man, a military officer in a red-and-gold uniform topped with a black-plumed shako, hurried to the King's side and bent his ear to the King's mouth to hear his whispered instructions. When he straightened, he bowed, then returned to stand stiffly behind the King again.

The King motioned to the Dean to continue his speech, and the Dean smoothly resumed. But David wasn't listening. He was watching the officer who had just retreated behind the King. The officer who was standing beside none other than Murdo Balfour. After a few moments, Murdo turned his head and whispered something in the man's ear. The military man reciprocated. Whatever Murdo heard made his eyebrows raise and his gaze seek out David, a funny little smile twisting up that mobile mouth. Then he nodded and looked away.

A few minutes later, the Dean concluded his speech and the faculty delegation was led aside by a frosty Sir Anthony, their places taken by the good Magistrates of Leith.

Chapter Eight

The ceremony finally ended at five o'clock. The King left the Entrée Room first, his entourage sweeping behind him. Only then did everyone else stir. Hats were removed and cravats pulled aside. Coat buttons undone. Men stretched and paced, shaking out muscles grown cramped and achy from the long afternoon.

The Dean didn't give in to the general relaxation of manners. He remained as tightly buttoned up as ever, his expression chilly as he offered the rest of the faculty delegation seats in his carriage. David declined the offer. He could walk home in scarcely half an hour, he replied, and besides, he'd welcome the exercise after the long stand. He watched the Dean carefully, wondering what the man had made of David's odd exchange with the King. It was impossible to say. The Dean didn't mention it, even when Braeburn came wheezing up to join them, congratulating David on his quick reactions as though the only reason no one else had stepped forward had been David's uncanny speed.

Well, when Chalmers had asked David to take his place, he'd wanted David to make an impression on his senior colleagues, and it seemed David had done so, though whether it was the right impression, he wasn't entirely sure.

David hung back as the men crowding the Entrée Room began to slowly shuffle out. He wasn't in a particular hurry to leave. There was the small matter of Murdo Balfour to consider after all. Murdo, whom David had agreed to meet again, despite his misgivings.

At the moment, however, there was no sign of the man. Murdo had followed the King out of the Entrée Room with the rest of the royal party, and for all David knew, he'd already left—a few minutes ago, the sound of coaches rumbling away over cobbles had filtered through the windows that looked out onto the courtyard, the sound of the King and his entourage returning to his temporary residence in Dalkeith.

David suppressed a sigh and joined the end of the line of men slowly filing out.

It was ten minutes later, just as David was leaving the Entrée Room, that he finally saw the man who dominated his thoughts. Murdo stood waiting just outside the big double doors, one broad shoulder leaning nonchalantly against the wall.

David pulled up short so suddenly the man behind him walked into the back of him.

"Ooof!"

David looked over his shoulder, apologising profusely and earning himself a filthy look from an elderly man wearing the black robes of the Kirk.

When he turned back to Murdo, the man had straightened up and, standing beside him, was the military officer the King had summoned to his side after his exchange with David. He was carrying his shako under his arm now, revealing a head of dark hair and a handsome countenance.

"Mr. Lauriston?" the officer said, surprising David by being the first to speak. "Do you have a moment?" He had merry blue eyes and a dashing moustache waxed into little points at the corners. Straight, very white teeth.

David looked between the two men, feeling a little dazed. Then, "Of course," he said, stepping towards them and away from the steady stream of men emerging from the Entrée Room.

Murdo's companion offered his hand. "Captain Iain Sinclair, at your service." David shook his hand and nodded. "And this is Lord Murdoch Balfour."

David glanced at Murdo, unsure how to play this. When Murdo murmured something about it being a pleasure, it was more effort than it ought to have been to keep his own expression neutral and make similar noises.

"The King asked me to speak to you," Captain

Sinclair said, dragging David's attention away from Murdo. "He was grateful to you for your—how did he put it?—your *good Scotch common sense*." Sinclair grinned at that, inviting David to enjoy the King's whimsy.

David smiled dutifully. "It was nothing," he replied, uncomfortable being thanked for such a trifle. "I would have done the same for anyone."

"Nevertheless, I am under strict instruction to invite you to the Peers' Ball this Friday evening, at His Majesty's particular request, in gratitude to you for services rendered to your sovereign." He grinned again, enjoying himself. Evidently this captain liked handing out the King's favours.

"How kind," David murmured. "But I'm sure I have another commitment that evening." It sounded like the lie it was, but David didn't much care. The thought of going to a ball was bad enough. A *peers'* ball sounded like torture.

Captain Sinclair wasn't to be so easily put off, though. "I'm afraid that won't do," he said, eyes twinkling. "Will it, Lord Murdo?"

"No, indeed," Murdo agreed gravely. "The King speaks, and we obey. He wishes you to attend, Mr. Lauriston—now Captain Sinclair and I must see that it happens."

"Or rather, Lord Murdo must," the captain said apologetically. "I am already taking care of several other of the King's personal favours that evening. But Lord Murdo here will see you are all kitted out if you require highland dress—we would not wish you to be uncomfortable, Mr. Lauriston—and he will escort you there in his personal carriage, won't you, Lord Murdo?"

"Like Mr. Lauriston's own fairy godmother," Murdo agreed dryly, and the captain chuckled.

"There is no need for that," David protested. "If it came to it, I have formal evening clothes, but I truly have another engagement—"

"My good fellow, it will not do for you to reject the King's kindness," Murdo interrupted him. "If Captain Sinclair hasn't convinced you, let me try. Come and I'll buy you an ale and set about persuading you to accept the King's invitation. Will you join us, Sinclair?"

The captain sighed. "I wish I could, but I'm to ride straight to Dalkeith after this. Can I leave you to take care of things with our new friend?"

"Consider it done," Murdo replied.

"Then I'll away. Mr. Lauriston." Sinclair clapped David on the shoulder. "It was a pleasure to meet you, sir. Pray, do not disappoint the King on Friday evening. He remembers these incidents, you know." He gave one last bright grin, turned on his heel and hurried away.

"That sounded like a threat," David murmured, watching the departing captain's uniformed back.

"No," Murdo replied in an amused voice. "He merely means that the King can become emotional when he feels let down, and it's tedious for those closest to him, like the good captain. You're perfectly at liberty not to attend if you truly don't wish to." He paused, then added more seriously, "But I hope you will come. It will brighten a very dull occasion for me."

David glanced up at that. An unfamiliar expression on Murdo's face made something in his chest shift and alter, a cliff edge crumbling into the sea. He couldn't find words to respond and had to look away. It was a relief when Murdo spoke again, his tone lighter.

"Let's go and have that ale. The tavern we went to last time—is it near your rooms?"

David glanced back at Murdo. His expression had changed. Now he was smiling again, his dark gaze promising.

That was easier. Better.

"Yes," David said. "Very near. I'll show you."

The same innkeeper welcomed them into the tavern. He found them a pair of stools, which they pulled up to the scarred wooden bar. There were no free tables today. The tavern was swollen with visitors to the city for the King's visit. They ordered ale and two plates of mutton stew.

It seemed that standing idly around at Holyrood Palace had been oddly hungry work—David polished off his stew quickly and gulped down the ale, agreeing to another tankard when Murdo suggested it.

Murdo told him tales of the King and his entourage while they ate and drank. Of the King's emotional nature and of his sometimes childish petulance. Of the foibles of his closest advisers. He spoke of who was truly influential and who was merely tolerated. He spoke about the King's adoration of his garish, frowsy mistress, Lady Conyngham, and of their absurd antics, often conducted in front of the lady's well-rewarded husband and children.

"You are shocked," Murdo observed, considering David's expression.

David realised his brows were indeed drawn together in a disapproving frown.

"Well, it is shocking, is it not?" he said. "When you think of the power and riches vested in such a man while ordinary people struggle and starve. Look at what he's spent on his pleasure palace in Brighton."

"I agree, it's appalling," Murdo said. "But even so, I would love to show it to you. In the banqueting room there's a chandelier that hangs from the claws of a great dragon. It's magnificent."

"It's a shocking waste," David said, even as he tried to picture that chandelier.

"Yes, it is," Murdo agreed, capturing David's gaze with his own. "But extraordinary nonetheless. Should we knock it down now because it ought never to have been built?"

"Perhaps we should."

"Says the man who stepped forward and stopped the King falling over today. Knowing full well what a profligate wastrel he is."

"He looked poorly," David said defensively. "I saw him sway and acted without thinking. I would have done the same for anyone."

"I know you would," Murdo said and smiled.

David didn't much like his actions being examined so closely. He cast around for a change of subject. "Tell me about Captain Sinclair," he said after a moment. "Is he a favourite of the King?"

"Ah, now he is an interesting one," Murdo replied. "He's fairly new to the King's circle and does not occupy an especially high position yet, but he is a man who hears all. There is something about him men like to confide in. They want him to like them, I think. They give him information to curry favour with him."

David thought of the man's comely form and bright gaze, his sharp uniform and handsome moustache. He could see what Murdo meant. Even a man who did not share their proclivities would admire Sinclair, with his confident masculinity and dashing appearance. He was the sort of man both men and women would be drawn to.

"Tell me something he has heard, then," David invited, a hint of challenge in his voice. "Something I could not know."

"You assume he would confide in me?" The beginnings of a smile played at the corner of Murdo's mouth.

"Some things, yes, or you couldn't know how much he learns. Besides, you seemed friendly—and he must trust you if he handed you the errand the King gave him."

"Getting you to the Peers' Ball, you mean? Perhaps I asked Sinclair to give that errand to me." Murdo smiled, but his face was unreadable. David wasn't sure if he preferred this Murdo, ambiguous and unsettling, or the one from earlier with his tender, unguarded gaze. Both incited feelings in David that were uncomfortable.

"All right, then," Murdo said, interrupting David's thoughts. "Here's something he told me. Have you heard about Lord Londonderry?"

"That he's dead? Yes."

The news of the Foreign Secretary's demise had only just arrived in Scotland. The man had taken his own life around the same time the King had set sail for Scotland.

David paused, then added, "I also heard that it was suicide."

Murdo inclined his head, acknowledging the accuracy of that statement. "He severed his own throat with a pocket knife."

David shuddered. "Christ—"

"Oh, but there's more—here's what Sinclair told me." He bent his head close to David's ear and said, his voice very low, "Londonderry went to see the King just before the King left for Scotland. He was raving. Told the King he was a fugitive of justice, that he'd been accused of the same crimes as the Bishop of Clogher. He was kissing the King's hand and begging his forgiveness one minute, then ranting like a madman the next."

David swallowed against the sudden nausea in his throat. The arrest last month of the Bishop of Clogher when he was caught in a compromising position with a grenadier guardsman in a public house had been the biggest scandal in years. All the more so when the bishop broke bail and disappeared. It had caught the public imagination, and it seemed to David that whenever the case came up, people spoke as though the crime of buggery was responsible for all the world's ills. As though the actions of two men in a private room could somehow leak out of windows and wall-cracks and infect everyone else with wickedness.

But then, was it so surprising people thought that way? It was what David had been brought up to believe, after all. And he *had* believed it. He'd been convinced that his fascination with the act, his desire for other men, was a sign of a weak and sinful nature. Something to be suppressed at all costs.

Had that changed? Had *he* changed?

It used to be, when he heard people sneering about *sods* and *buggers*, his chief reaction was shame. Self-loathing. But more recently—like when the scandal of the bishop came out—he'd found himself growing angry when he heard such comments. Angry that people seemed to think they had a right to know what others did behind closed doors. Angry that they wanted to rip people apart for it, even blamed the state of the nation upon it. That they assumed the men who did these acts were mad with a depraved sort of lust.

That they presumed to know how a man in that position *felt*—

"Are you quite all right?"

David started and found Murdo regarding him with a concerned expression.

"Yes—I'm fine," he said. "It's just such a horrible business. Londonderry, I mean."

Murdo frowned. "I oughtn't to have blurted it out like that. I forget sometimes that you're not like the people I usually circulate amongst."

Aristocrats, he meant. Aristocrats and politicians. People with power and influence.

"Wouldn't your friends have found it as shocking as I did?"

"I don't consider those people friends, and no, they'd have thought it a delicious bit of gossip."

"Oh." David wondered what Murdo inferred from that. That David was hopelessly naïve, perhaps?

"Look, do you want the rest of that ale?"

The unexpected change of subject set David back on his heels.

"Ah—not especially, no."

"Shall we leave, then?" Murdo sent David a sidelong look. "I'd like to see your rooms, if that would be all right."

David didn't hesitate for a moment. He put down his tankard and stepped off his stool. "All right. Let's go. They're only a few minutes' walk away."

Murdo's smile blossomed, quick and surprised. "Good," he said, as though he hadn't expected such easy agreement. "Good, that's good."

He turned his head, lifting his hand to catch the innkeeper's attention, and the man immediately came over to them, wiping his hands on his apron.

"Can I get you anythin' else, gents?"

"No, thank you." Murdo drew a handful of coin from his pocket and dropped it into the man's meaty palm without even checking what he was handing over. It was enough that no more need be said apparently. The innkeeper murmured his thanks and his hope that they would come again soon.

They jammed their hats on and left the cosy tavern, emerging into a night that was cool and somewhat misty.

"It's this way," David said, turning to walk up the hill. "On Castlehill."

"Let me speak to my coachman first," Murdo said. "I won't be a minute."

He sauntered over to where his carriage waited and passed a minute's conversation with the man sitting on the box.

As he walked back towards David, the horses began to move, the carriage rumbling away.

"Where is he going?" David asked when Murdo reached him. "You can't stay with me, I'm afraid—I only have one bed and my maid comes very early in the morning. And you can't possibly walk back to Queen Street dressed like that." He gestured at Murdo's exquisitely elegant clothes. "You'll be set upon."

"Don't worry," Murdo replied with an amused smile. "I've only sent him away for a few hours. He's coming back for me."

"Oh." David relaxed, relieved. "Well, in that case, follow me."

Chapter Nine

Murdo followed David up the worn stone stairs of the close that led to his rooms, waiting silently in the dark as David unlocked the front door before following him into the more profoundly dark interior.

Moving with the ease of long practice, David brushed past Murdo to lock up behind them, his fingers finding bolts and keyholes without needing to see them.

"Follow me," he said, stepping past Murdo to head down the hallway. "It's dark, but Ellen will have left a fire ready to be lit in the parlour, so we'll soon have light."

"Where the hell are you?" came Murdo's amused voice in reply, then a touch to David's shoulder as Murdo found him. His hand was warm and heavy, and when David turned his head, he was suddenly able to make out the faintest outline of Murdo's body standing opposite him, a dark shape amongst all the other shadows.

"Sorry. Here, give me your hand." David placed his

own on Murdo's, smiling when Murdo loosely entwined their fingers.

It was only a few steps down the hall to the parlour. David drew Murdo behind him, through the door and right into the depths of the room, carefully guiding him till he stood in front of his best armchair before giving him a gentle shove. Murdo yelped in surprise as he overbalanced, laughing as he hit the seat.

"Where are you now?" Murdo asked.

"Lighting the fire," David replied as he knelt before the grate, fumbling for the tinder box. "Not that I'd expect you to think of that. I don't suppose you've ever had to light a fire for yourself."

Murdo laughed again. "Not indoors," he admitted. "Though my brothers and I used to be fond of lighting them in the woods at home. Much to our tutor's dismay."

"Typical boys." David snorted, striking the flint to sprinkle sparks over the kindling. "That's just what William and I used to do."

"William's your brother?"

"No, my brother's called Drew. William was—a friend."

Murdo must've heard the pause. "Just a friend?"

"Yes, just a friend." David struck the flint again, bringing it closer to the kindling this time. "Though I mistook him for something else for a while."

Another shower of sparks, and another, then there

it was—a tiny tongue of flame, just licking at the kindling. David leaned forward and blew. A puff of encouragement.

"What kind of something else? A lover?"

David laughed shortly. "I was sixteen, so no, not that—not in my mind, anyway. I did believe I loved him, though. A platonic sort of love, you understand. Very noble. Very pure." He laughed again, mocking himself, and lifted the bellows, nurturing the infant flames with careful little gusts.

"Did he realise how you felt?"

Somehow it was easier to answer that deep, disembodied voice than if he'd been looking at Murdo.

"Oh, yes," David admitted. "I was a perfect fool and told him."

A pause, then, "What did he say?"

"Not much. He kissed me."

The silence that followed that admission was as profound as the darkness.

After a long time, Murdo's voice emerged, quiet and careful. "Was it your first kiss?"

"Yes. His too."

David sat back on his heels and regarded the fire. Already the flames were growing big and yellow, licking hungrily over the neat stack of wood and kindling that Ellen had built earlier. Those big flames were deceptive, though. This was exactly the moment when you had to watch a fire. As healthy as it looked now, once the kindling burned off, it could easily die without properly taking hold.

David stood and felt around on the mantelpiece for a candle, grabbing a sturdy, tallow one and bending to light the wick in the flames in the grate. Sheltering the flaring wick with his cupped hand, he carefully placed the candle in its holder and put it back on the mantelpiece before settling himself on the hearth rug again to keep an eye on the fire.

"I'll get you a drink in a minute," he promised, glancing over his shoulder at Murdo, who sprawled in David's best armchair like a pasha. "I'll just make sure I've got this fire going properly first."

"Don't worry about fetching me anything. I don't need a drink," Murdo replied. "Tell me more about this William instead."

David sighed, but after a moment, he said, "He was the boy from the big house. I used to see him whenever he was home from boarding school. We were playmates when we were children."

"When did you decide you were in love with him? Before or after you realised you preferred men?"

"After, I think. Though I didn't really think of it as being 'in love' with him."

"How did you think of it?"

"As an idealised sort of love, I suppose. I thought of us like David and Jonathan in the Bible." David stared into the flames in the grate. "I think I had the idea that if I ignored my physical desires, it would be all right to feel that way. William and I would be friends all our lives, and I would love him better than anyone else, more than any wife could ever love him." He laughed, and it was an ugly sound.

"But it didn't work out that way?"

Another short laugh. "No."

David blew a few more strategic puffs from the bellows and watched as the yellow flames intensified, growing longer and bolder, eating up the kindling quickly.

"Yet it was he who kissed you? Not the other way round?"

"The first time we kissed, it was him."

"It wasn't just once, then?"

David looked over his shoulder. There was no real heat coming from the fire yet, but it was throwing off some light now. Together with the light from the candle, it sent a glow about the room that made Murdo, in his armchair, discernible, though only barely. David could make out the outline of that big, lounging body and the sprawl of those long, careless limbs. His face, though, remained shrouded in shadow.

"Three times," he admitted, adding, "On the third occasion, we were discovered by my father."

"Ah."

That single syllable fairly thrummed with understanding.

David turned back to the fire, applying the bellows again. This time when he was done, it was burning merrily. He put the bellows aside and stood up.

"How about some whisky?" he said brightly, moving to the sideboard where he kept a decanter of the stuff. The need for some hard spirit was agitating him suddenly.

"What happened with your father after he found you with William?" Murdo asked, ignoring David's question.

David sloshed an inch of the hard stuff into a glass. "It wasn't so bad, considering what he saw. He didn't disown me. Nothing like that." He threw back the spirit he'd poured in one gulp and filled the glass again. "Are you sure you won't join me?"

Again Murdo ignored him. "If he didn't disown you, what happened?"

David shrugged. "Demanded an explanation. William—well, he put the blame on me. When I wouldn't deny it, my father knocked me down." He fingered his jaw, remembering that. The only time his father had ever struck him, and it had been the sort of punch a man throws at another man, fuelled by rage and insult, no holds barred. One minute David had been standing, pleading with the old man; the next he'd been on the ground, staring up at his gentle father in shock.

"Then he marched up to the big house, demanding to see William's father," David continued. "I don't know what was said, but the next day William was sent away to Oxford. And that was all. It was never mentioned again." He gulped down the second measure of whisky, and, as usual, the second nip felt twice as mellow as the first. Easier in every way. "The worst part was knowing how badly I'd let my father down."

That wasn't true. The worst part had been being betrayed by William.

Murdo was silent for a long time. "Come here," he said at last.

The shadow that was Murdo opened his legs and beckoned David with a tilt of his chin. When David stepped into the space between his thighs, Murdo reached for him, his hands going to David's hips and pulling him in closer.

The glow of the fire played across the planes of Murdo's face. He wore an odd expression, a softness about his dark eyes as he watched David.

David stood there, waiting for the next question, or maybe another assessment of David's character. No doubt this would be more grist to the mill of Murdo's theory about David's inability to enjoy the pleasures that Murdo so easily revelled in.

But when he spoke, all Murdo said was, "What do you want?"

"What? What do you mean?"

By way of answer, Murdo shifted, sitting up, leaning forward to place his hand on the crotch of David's breeches, his fingers tracing the shape of David's cock, shocking it into hardness. "Tell me what you want."

"Me?"

Murdo gave a soft gust of laughter. "Yes, you. So far, I've always led and you've followed. Tonight, you decide."

David balked. He'd never done such a thing. Never been the one to take the lead.

Except, no. There had been one time. That last day with William, behind the stables. He'd reached for William and had drawn him forward, bringing their mouths together. His heart had been so full, and it was like happiness and pain together. Almost unbearable. The sun had been warm on David's bare head, and he'd had William's lips on his, his strong, young body in David's arms.

And then his father had come.

He wanted that again, that innocent happiness, untainted by the world's disapproval. He wanted it, even knowing it was unobtainable.

"Kiss me," he begged. The hoarseness of his own voice surprised him, the edge of emotion audible. Embarrassed, he cleared his throat, sounding calmer when he added, "I want you to kiss me."

Murdo stood, his body brushing against David's as he rose. He was taller than William, broader, a man, not a youth. There wasn't a bit of innocence or purity in him. He was sinful and cynical. Unapologetic. He cared nothing for the world. He just ate its fruits and roamed its wilds and didn't need anyone. This kiss would be nothing like that long-ago one.

Murdo lowered his head, tilting David's chin up with one finger. The odd expression from earlier was back, the one that made David feel raw. He closed his eyes, but he couldn't do anything about the heart that was pounding in his chest.

Murdo's lips touched his own, feather-light, just a ghost of a kiss, while one hand drifted into David's hair, cupping the back of his head. He gave a hum of pleasure and did it again, and again, slowly deepening the kiss. His lips, warm and pliable, made seductive little passes at David's mouth until, at last, he took possession of it completely, pressing his tongue inside, one powerful arm tightening around David's torso, drawing him in close.

David felt something inside him crack, the banked-up lust inside him flooding out. He wrapped his arms round the other man's neck, opening his mouth and meeting Murdo's tongue with his own, his breathing coming suddenly hard.

He was right. This kiss was nothing like that long-ago one. There was no fooling himself as to what this was. He and Murdo were not loving friends. They were not, and would never be, a David and Jonathan. Murdo wanted him. And every time they came together, it felt easier, more natural.

David tore his mouth away from Murdo's, panting. "I want you to fuck me."

The word—*fuck*—from his lips sounded harsh, brutal, but it was honest too. Finally, David giving voice to the deep-seated desire that had tormented him for so long.

Murdo went very still. "I'm not sure that's a good idea."

The words were like cold water. David dropped his hands from Murdo's shoulders, stepping back. Mortification scalded his cheeks.

"David..." Murdo reached for him again. "David—please. It's not that I don't want to. Christ, I want to so badly, it hurts. You *must* know that!"

"Must I?" He bit the words out, humiliated.

Murdo let out a huff of frustration, passing a hand over his face. "For once in my life—for *once*—I try to do the right thing—"

"What do you mean by that?"

"I mean that fucking you, for the first time in your life, just after you've told me all about the love of your life, the man who let you down and betrayed you in front of your father, is not a good idea. I can't—it doesn't feel right."

"Why?" David snapped. "I want it, Murdo. I *do*."

"Because I don't want to do it when you're thinking about bloody *William*, all right? And I want the first time we do this…if there ever is a first time…to be…to be…" He broke off, seeming lost for words suddenly.

"What? Tell me."

Murdo sighed. "Gentle."

"*Gentle?*"

"Yes." This was delivered through gritted teeth.

"Christ, Murdo, I'm not some virgin girl on her wedding night! I'm six-and-twenty, and I've sucked more cocks in back alleys than I care to remember. I don't need gentle. Christ, I don't *deserve* gentle."

For a moment, Murdo just stared at him, and his dark gaze was furious. David had the sinking sense he'd said something terribly wrong. He braced himself for Murdo to explode with anger, but instead Murdo turned aside and drove his fist into the wall.

"*Jesus Christ!*" David yelled. "What the hell are you doing?" He rushed to Murdo's side and grabbed his arm to examine his hand. Murdo's hand shook, and all the knuckles were split and bleeding. He tore it out of David's grip.

David looked at the wall. "You've cracked the plaster!"

"Sorry," Murdo muttered. "I'll have it fixed."

"That's not what I meant, I just meant—Christ, your *hand*, Murdo! What were you thinking? What did I say?" He loosened the knot of his own cravat and drew it off, gently wrapping it round Murdo's knuckles.

"You said that you didn't deserve me to be gentle with you."

David looked up from securing the linen round Murdo's injured hand. "But why—"

Murdo swallowed. "It brought back memories," he said, and his gaze was bleak.

"Let's sit down," David murmured. He guided Murdo back to the armchair and pressed him into it, but when he went to take the chair on the other side of the fireplace, Murdo captured his hand and tugged at it.

"Sit here with me," he said.

David paused. "How?"

"Here, on my lap."

David gave an awkward laugh. "I'm not a woman—" he began.

"For Christ's sake, David!" Murdo cried. "I *know* you're not a woman! If I wasn't aware of it already, I'd certainly know from how often you remind me! Can't you just sit with me because I want you near me?" His voice carried despair and frustration, and David felt suddenly ashamed.

"Oh, all right," he said reluctantly.

He lowered himself, somewhat awkwardly, till he was sitting on Murdo's lap, his back against the other man's chest. Behind him, Murdo let out a soft gust of laughter, his deep voice reverberating in his chest.

Then he murmured, "Thank you," in David's ear, and his arms came around David's chest, tugging him a little closer.

For a while, they stayed like that, David's stiffness gradually leaving him till at last he lounged, relaxed, against the other man. The fire crackled merrily now, the flames mesmerising. Behind David, Murdo's big body was warm and powerful, responsive. Hard, but with give in it too. Strangely comforting, which was surely wrong when David should be the one giving comfort. Shouldn't he?

It was almost a shock when Murdo finally spoke.

"My first time was not gentle," he began in a quiet voice. "I was—badly used. There were two of them, and they were rough with me. I was only nineteen."

"Christ," David whispered. "Murdo, I'm so sorry, I didn't realise."

"I was stupid," Murdo said, shaking his head. "And very naïve. I trusted someone I ought to have known better than to trust."

"You are not to blame for others' brutality."

"I know that. But I know too what it is to be taken, for the first time, in a way that is not gentle. To be used, like a thing. I do not want that for you."

"It wouldn't be like that between us."

"I know. But it's not just that. I want it to be perfect."

"Perfect? What would be perfect?"

"You and me, both wanting it fully, both certain."

"I *am* certain."

"I'm not sure you are. It's no accident you're asking for this after telling me about William and your father. You were upset—"

"I'm fine," David interrupted.

"Yes, I could see that by the way you poured yourself half a gallon of whisky and drank it down like you were dying of thirst."

David closed his eyes, suddenly aware of the taste of the spirit in his mouth. He was glad Murdo sat behind him, unable to see his face. "I do want you, though," he whispered.

"Do you?"

"God, yes. I ache." Inside him, a chasm of wanting yawned, both physical and not.

Murdo's uninjured hand had been resting on David's chest, but now he began to move it slowly downwards, stopping only when he reached the placket of David's breeches. He stroked David's shaft through the fabric in an unhurried way, tracing the shape of it with his fingers and bringing it quickly back to full hardness. David gave a soft moan and bucked his hips up into the air, needing more.

"Take it out for me," Murdo breathed in his ear. "I want to see it."

David obeyed, fiddling with the buttons until his breeches were open, drawing his cock out of his smallclothes. He was almost painfully hard now, his shaft ruddy in the firelight.

"Hmmm," Murdo murmured, approval in the low sound. "Now let me see how you pleasure yourself when you're alone."

David leaned back a bit more, letting his head drop into the space between Murdo's neck and shoulder. He took his cock in hand and began to stroke up and down in the familiar rhythm he used on himself.

"God in heaven, you're gorgeous," Murdo said after a while, his voice rough. "I want to see more of you."

He deftly unbuttoned David's waistcoat and peeled the garment from his shoulders, then grabbed handfuls of his shirt and hauled it up and over David's head, tossing it aside to join the waistcoat on the floor.

Now David's upper body was naked and his breeches and smallclothes were open, displaying his turgid shaft and tight balls and the springy, copper-tinged curls framing them.

Murdo shifted below him, bringing both arms around David's body. He anchored his injured hand round David's waist while he ran the other hand restlessly over David's chest. His fingers brushed David's nipples, lingering when David moaned, teasing the small buds gently and pinching them sweetly. The pleasure that simple attention elicited was absurdly intense, as though a wire connected David's nipples to his balls. He arched up, wanting more. Murdo laughed softly and obliged him, turning his head to nuzzle the side of David's neck. The scrape of his rough cheek against the soft flesh there was exquisite, the press of his hot mouth too.

"Keep stroking yourself," Murdo muttered, bucking his own hips up against David's buttocks so that David couldn't miss that he too was intensely aroused.

David obeyed, tugging at his swollen shaft, his hand working more quickly now, the pleasure building in his cock, his balls.

"God, yes, that's it. You need this so badly, don't you? You can't wait. Let me see you come all over yourself."

And suddenly David was coming, crying out as he climaxed, his hot seed spattering his belly and chest, one drop landing shoulder-high, making Murdo laugh softly. "Oh you eager boy!"

When he was all wrung out, David lay, panting on top of Murdo, letting the slowly receding waves of pleasure ebb away, letting Murdo's caressing hands and murmuring praise ease him back to the world.

Murdo's own unfulfilled desire pressed underneath him, demanding and undeniable. David shifted, turning a little.

"Shall I suck you?" he asked.

Murdo's eyes glittered. "Yes, but stay like this awhile longer. I like you here."

So David did, enjoying the warmth of the fire and

the feel of Murdo beneath him, around him. Enjoying the tentative intimacy that was growing between them and that felt almost tangible, here, in this warm, secret corner of the world.

Chapter Ten

Tuesday, 20th August, 1822

Parliament House was deserted, the faculty library as bare of living souls as Greyfriars cemetery. David was the only man in the place. Even old Mr. McGilchrist, who'd sat at the same desk every day for the last thirty years, wasn't in today.

The celebrations for the King's visit seemed to have overtaken the city to such an extent that the ordinary everyday business of living, including the work of the courts, had ground to a halt.

It was a good day to catch up on work, though, and David had much to catch up on. Three opinions to write and a petition to draft by the end of the week. Strange to think that it wasn't so very long ago that he'd been worried about where his next case was coming from.

Chalmers's patronage had changed that completely. Not only did he get a steady stream of work from Chalmers himself, several of the solicitors who instructed Chalmers had taken to engaging him directly. And the cases he was being used for were getting bigger, more valuable, more complicated. More satisfying. Mr. Russell of Guild & Russell, one of the busiest firms in the city, had even proposed David to join Russell's exclusive private club as soon as a space became available, and whilst David would never have sought membership for himself, there was no doubt it was pleasing to be asked. His sudden success—as unexpected as it was longed for—was heady. But he certainly had to work hard for it.

Without Donald Ferguson around to badger him to eat, David worked past the hour at which he usually ate luncheon and well into the afternoon, entirely caught up in answering the questions posed in Russell's latest memorial. It was only when one of the library clerks touched his shoulder that he finally looked up from his books.

"Sorry to interrupt you, Mr. Lauriston, but there's a gentleman asking for you. A Mr. MacLennan."

David blinked his surprise. He hadn't expected another visit, not after Euan's hasty departure from his rooms.

"Is he waiting in the hall?" David asked, wincing as he straightened. Hours of stooping over books had left him stiff.

"Yes, sir."

"All right, thank you, I'll go and see him now. Would you replace these volumes for me?"

The clerk's eyebrows rose to see the size of the pile of books David was referring to, but he agreed readily enough, and David left his desk, abandoning his scattered notes where they lay.

He made his way out the bowels of the library and entered Parliament Hall, his footsteps echoing as he crossed the empty floor to the man who stood at the other end, his hands linked behind his back as he contemplated a marble bust of some judge of the last century.

The last time Euan had come to this building looking for David, he'd been a boy, self-conscious of his lanky height and twisting his hat in his hands. Today, he was someone else entirely. He stood tall and broad and confident, smartly clothed and clean-shaven. A respectable man of the world.

He smiled as David drew closer, holding out his hand. "Davy, it's good to see you again."

David shook the proffered hand, watching Euan carefully. "And you. What can I do for you?"

"I'm afraid I was very rude the other day, at your rooms. Rushing off that like that, I mean." Euan offered an apologetic smile. "I was in a hurry, but it's no excuse. Will you let me buy you a dram to make up for it?" His expression was open, the regret in his gaze sincere.

"I've rather a lot of work to do," David replied, thinking of Murdo's warnings, then felt a stab of guilt.

"Can't you spare me an hour?" Euan asked. "I wanted to let you know about Peter."

David paused. "You've news?"

Peter, Euan's brother, had been transported to the Antipodes for treason two years before. David had always wondered if he'd survived the journey.

"Better than that." Euan smiled. "I got a letter from him, a few months ago now. Come on, Davy, even if you're busy, you can spare me an hour, can't you? We'll go to the Tolbooth Tavern like we used to, but this time I'll buy your whisky."

Curiosity about Peter—and perhaps a kind of foolish loyalty to Euan—won over wisdom.

"All right," David said. "You go ahead. I'll meet you there in twenty minutes."

"Good." Euan's smile became a grin. "I'll see you there."

Euan took his leave, and David went back to the library to tidy his papers. Though he packed his notes away, he left his satchel at his desk. He would come back here to work on later. A few drams wouldn't affect his concentration. Indeed, sometimes it felt like he worked better with the mellow glow he got from whisky.

Donning his hat for the sake of respectability, David set off for the Tolbooth Tavern. It was only a few minutes down the High Street, and soon he was opening the door and stepping inside.

It was busy inside, but Euan had managed to secure them a nook by one of the windows, just a bit of ledge to sit on and a small rough table. He waved at David, beckoning him over.

When David got there, he saw that Euan had already bought the drink. A little earthenware jug of whisky sat, waiting to be poured into a small pewter cup. Euan himself was drinking ale. David wondered if it was still his habit to avoid the spirits his older brother had so disapproved of.

"You came," Euan said, smiling.

"Of course. I said I would, didn't I?" David squeezed into the narrow window seat beside the other man and poured himself a measure of the hard stuff. He took a gulp. It was rough and fiery. Very far from the best whisky he'd ever tasted, but still, that burn was an old, familiar friend.

"You're a man of your word," Euan agreed.

"I like to think so," David replied, taking his hat off and laying it on the table. "So, what news of your brother?"

Euan reached into the inside pocket of his coat and drew out a paper. "Read for yourself," he said, handing it to David.

"Are you sure?"

"Yes, go on."

David unfolded the letter and began to read Peter's neat, copperplate handwriting. The tone of it was typical of the man, pithy and understated. He hadn't had to suffer "too many floggings" on his arrival, he said. And though the first year had been "unpleasant", he'd finally been assigned to a "good master" who appreciated his skills and literacy. Now he was foreman at the man's works, and was married.

"Married!" David exclaimed, looking up.

Euan grinned—really grinned this time. "Can you imagine it? My bachelor brother with a woman?"

David gave a laugh. Peter had not been near as handsome as his younger brother, and though big and capable and a passionate radical, had been oddly shy with women. Perhaps the conditions of New South Wales gave a woman a different view of what was important in a husband. Or perhaps it gave a man a different view of himself.

"It sounds as though he's making the best of it," David said, folding the letter up and handing it back.

"Yes," Euan agreed as he tucked it away again. "I think he is. Though I know that when he says the first year was bad that it must have been truly horrible. And the thought of Peter having to suffer one of those brutal floggings you hear about—" He swallowed. "I can only hope this Mr. Munroe will keep him on."

"It sounds promising that he will," David pointed out. "I'll warrant this Monroe chap has seen what a steady character Peter is and how profitable he can be to the man's business."

A little of the worry faded from Euan's eyes. "You're right," he said firmly. "Peter would be an asset to anyone."

David lifted his cup in a toast. "To Peter," he said.

"To Peter," Euan repeated, lifting his tankard. They clicked rims and drank deeply.

After a brief silence, David asked, "And what of Peter's hopes for you?"

The letter had ended with Peter exhorting Euan not to give up his dreams of the Kirk, to try to complete his education.

Euan shrugged. "I wrote back straightaway, so he should know by now that I've become a journalist and won't ever be a minister of the Kirk."

"Will he mind, do you think?"

"I think he'll be as proud as a cockerel. He was never much of a churchgoer anyway. No, his next quest will probably be to persuade me to marry too."

David laughed. "And is there a lady who has your eye?"

Euan didn't answer straightaway. He looked down into his ale as though considering what to say, and when he raised his gaze again, he still didn't seem sure.

"There is someone," he admitted. "But she is beyond me."

"Her position, you mean?"

"That, and her marital state."

A married woman. Now, that was unwise, but

when had Euan ever been wise?

"You know her."

David looked at Euan sharply. "I know her? Who—"

The name that occurred to him, that made him break off mid-sentence, was confirmed by Euan in his next breath.

"Lady Kinnell."

"What?" David exclaimed. "But you've barely spoken to her."

"I know." Euan shook his head and gave a hopeless laugh. "It's ridiculous, isn't it?"

"I wouldn't say ridiculous precisely, but you met her for the first time just days ago and—"

"It was the second time I saw her," Euan interrupted.

"Sorry?"

"It was the second time I saw her."

"She looked at you like you'd hung the moon in the sky for her. I was sure she was in love with you. I thought you were a lucky dog."

"The ball at the Assembly Rooms," David said slowly, understanding dawning.

"Yes." Euan's cheeks reddened, and he added almost defiantly, "Don't you believe in love at first sight?"

"Is that what happened to you?" David asked. "You fell in love with her that night, two years ago? Just from seeing her?"

"Is it so unbelievable? Yes, I fell, right there."

"You didn't give any sign."

"I was rather preoccupied at the time, if you remember," Euan replied. "At the time, I was expecting to be on the run for murder rather imminently. Developing a romantic attachment to an unattainable, wealthy young lady was something of an inconvenience."

"And now?"

Euan let out a sigh and leaned back till his head touched the glass of the window behind him. "I didn't expect to see her ever again. I'd convinced myself it was a boy's foolishness and put it from my mind. She was the last person I expected to come across when I went to see you the other day."

"And now you learn she's married," David mused.

Euan's jaw tightened. "To a brute who mistreats her."

David sighed. "We don't know that for sure."

"I do."

"Just because we saw some bruises—"

"I asked her outright," Euan interrupted. "When you were seeing to your other guests."

"You asked her?" David couldn't disguise his incredulity. "What did you say?"

"I said, 'Did your husband put those bruises on the back of your neck?'" He paused. "She looked petrified and said he didn't mean to, and I said it didn't look like that. And then I started telling her about Mr. and Mrs. Gilmour—that was when you came back."

He should've known that Euan wouldn't leave his suspicions unspoken.

"I followed her home after," Euan continued. "That's why I left you in such a hurry. I didn't want to lose her trail."

"You *what*?"

"I followed her," Euan repeated, defiant. "I was worried for her, so I followed her, and I've seen them together, and he's just what you'd think, Davy. Cold and forbidding—she fears him. You can see it, just in the little ways they are together. I saw him criticising and berating her as they walked out their house and got into a carriage together. It took him less than a minute to have her quaking."

"You should not be following her!"

"She needs help."

"You are a…a known radical." David paused before adding, "If the authorities see you following a peer's wife around, they will think you plan some—some political scheme. They will arrest you."

Euan reared back in surprise at that. "The authorities? What do mean, *the authorities*?"

David turned his attention to pouring himself more whisky, unable to look Euan in the eye when he couldn't admit what he knew. "I've heard it said there are government men up from London tailing known troublemakers. I'm quite sure you fall into that category."

"It seems like a lot of bother to go to over someone like me. I've no convictions—"

"Your brother was convicted of treason, and you write for a radical paper that has expressed republican views. The King is here. Peel himself and many of his men too. Peel will take no chance over the King's safety, you can be sure, or his own. You should be prudent."

Euan huffed out a frustrated sigh. "You're right, I know. It's just—it's difficult for me to believe that Peel's men would think me worth watching when I know how little my efforts achieve. The more I want to see the world change, the more it seems to stay the same."

"The very fact that the government wants to close down *Flint's* should tell you that you're having more of an effect than you may think."

Euan thought about that, then nodded. "All right. I'll be extra careful around Lady Kinnell."

David sighed. "That's not what I mean, and you know it. You should stop following her altogether."

"I can't. I need to find a way of telling her that I'm willing to help her."

"Help how?"

"Any way she needs, preferably by getting her away

from her husband. The trouble is, she's hardly ever alone. He keeps her chaperoned all the time. She's like a prisoner."

David remembered the footman who'd come to his door. He hadn't liked the look of him.

Had Chalmers been subjected to that too? Visits from his daughter with her stony-faced guard in tow? Elizabeth had always been so bright and merry. It was awful to see her downtrodden like this. And yet—did they know what she herself thought of her situation? "How can you be sure she *wants* to escape her husband?" David asked.

"I can't," Euan said shortly. "She's had no chance to express a view. But I've eyes in my head. I see she's unhappy."

David thought of his Aunt Mamie back in Midlauder, the one who came knocking at his mother's door on Saturday nights looking for a safe haven from her drunk husband, then insisted on going back to him each Sunday morning. "And what if you're wrong?" he said. "What if she wants to stay with Kinnell and you're caught hanging around trying to speak to her? You could make him angry with her. It could make things worse for her."

"You think I haven't thought of that?" Euan exclaimed. "Of course I have! But I've also wondered if she's trapped with him, desperate to leave. Desperate to leave and unable to tell anyone."

David flinched at the thought of gentle Elizabeth being terrorised. He thought of the smiling, confiding girl he'd first met, and how sad and reserved she seemed now. "All I'm saying is that we would have to be certain. She is his wife. He has rights over her we can do nothing about. We could inadvertently cause her more harm if we are too hasty. We need to find out what Elizabeth thinks before we do anything else."

Euan gave a frustrated sigh. "This is not how marriage should be, with man exercising dominion over woman, like a master over a slave. It's obscene."

"I agree, but it is how things are. We must be practical."

"*Be practical*," Euan spat. Then he sighed and passed a hand over his face. "I realise I have to be careful. But I hate being told to be practical. It's what people always say when they mean you must put up with injustice and oppression."

"Injustice and oppression won't go away just because you want them to. Sometimes you have to find a way of working around them. Take this client I have just now—Annie. When her husband died, she discovered he was a bigamist. That meant her marriage was void and her baby was illegitimate and they had no claim on the man's estate as his wife and child. Now, I can't change the law for Annie, but I *can* help her by suing the estate in her father's name."

"You shouldn't have to do that, though."

"I know, but my point is that to help individuals, sometimes we have to work within the bounds of how things are, not how we would want them to be."

"And *my* point is that to overcome the injustice you've described, we can't just pragmatically help people one by one. We have to change the system. We have to win the battle of ideas. We have to give people new ideas to aspire to, ideas to replace the old ones. We have to say, *this is wrong; this must change.*"

"And that's how we stop men wanting to enslave their wives? By inspiring them with new ideas?" David's scepticism showed in his voice, he knew. But Euan seemed undaunted.

"No! By inspiring the wives! Imagine a world where every child was brought up by parents who loved and respected one another equally; who shared the work of the household and its fruits fairly. Don't you think those children would grow up more willing to be fair to their friends and neighbours? Our closest relationships are tainted with oppression and fear, when they should be about love and respect."

David felt an ache in his chest. His own parents loved one another. There had never been violence between them. A few angry words here and there, but soon made up. And that respect they had for one another was mirrored in all their dealings with their two sons and neighbours and friends. He felt a sudden yearning for them at that thought, a pang of longing for the simple goodness of his own family.

"Do you know what the ancients did, Davy? They made up regiments of lovers. Men who would fight side by side, both for themselves and for their lovers. They knew that such armies were invincible. Because as strong as hatred is—and it is very strong, I do not underestimate it—love is stronger. A man will fight for hate for a long time, but he will fight for love to the death. We are at our most noble when we love."

David stared at the younger man, taking in the belief that shone in his eyes. The way he spoke of armies of lovers—*male lovers*—without blinking an eye. The way he put love above everything else, above the institution of marriage and the laws of God and of man too.

Murdo Balfour had once accused David of being an idealist, but he was no such thing. Euan MacLennan was the real thing, and he awed David with his faith.

David, however, was a pragmatist to his very soul. He had said he would help Elizabeth, and he would.

"All right, listen to me," he said. "I will try to speak to Elizabeth privately. I will tell her we're willing to help her—you and I—if she wants to be helped."

"You mean it?" Euan asked, his gaze very intent. "You will help her too, if you can?"

"If I can, yes. We are not the only ones concerned about her, you know. Her father is too. He asked me to look out for her, and I promised that I would."

"But how will you get her alone? She is always chaperoned or with Kinnell. Is there any chance you might see her somewhere neutral, since you know her father? At his house perhaps?"

"From what Chalmers has said, I don't think Kinnell allows her to visit him alone, but there may be another chance. I've been invited to the Peers' Ball on Friday, and she may be there. If so, I'll try to speak with her alone."

"That sounds promising. If she wants to leave him, you can tell her that I have undertaken to personally get her safely out of Scotland and take her somewhere Kinnell will not find her. I've had to learn to cover my tracks over the years, and I have friends who will gladly help a woman in trouble make a new life." He paused. "But she has to be willing to take that chance."

"I'll tell her," David promised. "I only hope she's at this ball, because I struggle to see any other way of speaking with her privately."

"There will be a way," Euan said determinedly. "We'll think of something else if this doesn't work."

David nodded, but the truth was, if there was another way, he couldn't see it.

Chapter Eleven

Friday, 23rd August, 1822

David wore his usual evening clothes for the Peers' Ball: black evening coat and trousers, pristine white linen and an ivory satin waistcoat. This last was the most luxurious item of clothing he'd ever owned. When his fingers brushed the fabric, the heavy silkiness reminded him of when he was small and used to pet Fletch, his father's sheepdog, in front of the kitchen hearth. The dog's ears had felt like that, only warm. Warm and satiny.

His father used to say, *"You'll spoil that dog."*

He checked his appearance in the looking glass—the knot of his cravat looked all wrong. He loosened it and began again, but his second and third attempts were no better. The linen was all wilted now, the starch gone out of it. Impatient, he tied a simpler knot on his fourth attempt and decided it would do. It wasn't as though he was a fashionable young buck. Far from it. He was exactly what he looked like: a solid, professional man, overly sober in his dress and predictable in his habits.

Who would look at him and guess what he was? A sodomite. Or almost a sodomite. Certainly in thought, if not quite yet in deed.

Not quite yet.

He went out the front door and locked up, trying hard not to dwell on the fact that he may not return this night. A dozen things could get in the way of him spending another night with Murdo, and he dared not get his hopes up. Instead he thought of what he'd say to Elizabeth if he saw her. How he'd phrase an invitation to dance with her husband looking on.

He had plenty of time to ponder it. The walk to Murdo's house took longer than usual thanks to the crowds in George Street. The whole area around the Assembly Rooms was already congested with milling spectators and soldiers, and this over an hour before the ball was due to begin. Once past George Street, though, the streets were emptier, and soon enough, he was rapping on Murdo's front door.

He expected to be shown the way to Murdo's rooms, but this time the footman ushered him into a drawing room on the ground floor, taking his greatcoat and hat away and murmuring that his lordship would be with David presently. The man's accent gave him away as one of Murdo's London servants.

This room was much more formal than Murdo's private sitting room, the furniture more elegant, less comfortable. David brushed his hands over the tails of his coat before perching on a chair upholstered in black-and-gold-striped silk that looked far too fine to sit on.

His gaze wandered over the room, taking in the spare, masculine style of the décor. The furnishings were largely monochromatic, with just a few touches of gold here and there. Above the black marble fireplace hung a portrait of Murdo, standing in an improbably classical grove of trees, a pair of hunting dogs at his feet. Curious, David got to his feet to take a closer look. Though it was a good likeness, he didn't think it quite did Murdo justice. It missed his spark, the quick brightness of his gaze.

"There you are."

David started and turned on his heel to discover the subject of the painting in the flesh, standing in the doorway in full highland dress.

No tartan trews this time, but a full kilt in the Balfour colours of dark green and blue, complete with rabbit-fur sporran and matching tartan stockings gartered at the knee. Murdo had added a bit of reserved London style in the form of a black, short-waisted jacket, albeit with lace spilling from his throat and cuffs. With his height, broad shoulders and dramatic colouring, he looked like the hero from some romantic novel of Sir Walter's, right down to the silver *sgian dubh* protruding from his right stocking.

Before David could speak, Murdo strode into the room. "What are you wearing?" he said, coming to a stop an arm's length away, his frowning gaze taking in David's sober garb. "I'm sure I told you it was highland or court dress this evening, and you insisted you'd be fine."

David's irritation overcame his nerves. "You did, and I am," he said shortly. "I told you I had formal evening clothes. These are they, and they're perfectly adequate for the Assembly Rooms."

Murdo glanced up at his snappish tone, meeting David's gaze with an amused look "I should've known," he said. "I don't suppose the thought of looking out of place even troubles you?"

David stared at him, bewildered, and Murdo seemed to take that as confirmation of his point. He sighed. "I suppose I'll just have to persuade the Ball Committee to let you in notwithstanding."

"I didn't ask to come tonight," David pointed out.

"No," Murdo conceded, his tone even. "You didn't."

"And doesn't an invitation from the King himself count for anything?" David asked. He raised a teasing eyebrow, hiding the sudden concern that gripped him—that he might miss out on the chance to speak with Elizabeth purely because of his own stubborn refusal to comply with the dress code imposed by the Ball Committee.

"I suspect the King's personal invitation will get you in, if it comes to that." Murdo smiled, his gaze travelling over David again, more slowly this time. "And you look very well, I must say, in your black and white. Beau Brummel himself would approve, though"—he stepped closer and flipped the limp knot of linen at David's throat with one long finger—"I don't suppose he'd think much of your cravat."

David couldn't suppress the smile that sprang to his lips at Murdo's sudden nearness. "No," he admitted. "I don't suppose he would."

"Ironically enough, you'll be the most English-looking Scot in the room."

"I'll be the most *modern*-looking Scot," David corrected. "A professional man of the modern age."

"Ah. Is that why you don't want to wear tartan?" Murdo asked, a mischievous glint in his eye. "Doesn't it fit with your advocate persona?"

"That's not the reason at all," David retorted. "I don't want to wear tartan because my people don't wear it. I'm a lowlander. A Scots lowlander."

Murdo rolled his eyes at that. "David Lauriston," he sighed. Merely that, as though it was all the explanation he needed.

David's brows drew together with irritation. "It's a serious point."

"If you say so."

"It *is*. For me to wear a kilt—it would be..." He

thought, trying to pinpoint what it was that troubled him about it. "An...an insult."

Murdo sent him that mocking, amused look that David was so familiar with. "An insult to whom? To you?"

Perhaps it was the dismissive tone in Murdo's voice that riled him. Or perhaps it was the fact that Murdo was done up in a set of decorative regalia that, handsome as he looked in it, might have been designed by Sir Walter himself. Whatever it was, David felt a sudden stab of pure annoyance. He looked the other man over, from the tumble of snowy lace at his throat to the toes of his satin dancing slippers, then back up to meet his dark eyes.

"Yes," he said. "An insult to me. And to the people it means something to—not people like you, but the ordinary highlanders it was taken from. The people who were forbidden to wear it for such a long time."

Murdo's smile faded, and that fortified David.

"Come on, Murdo," he continued. "You must all know about that. You're a highlander, aren't you? The son of the laird himself. Did your father evict any of his tenants from their homelands to make room for sheep? Burn down any houses? Most of the chiefs did, I believe. In fact, some of the ones who are the most—"

"Stop it—"

"—sentimental about the old highland ways were the worst. We were lucky in the lowlands, by comparison. It was industry that cleared our lands and sent our people overseas. Cold comfort I suppose, but marginally better than being burned off the land by troops to make way for animals—"

"David, stop! Please."

David fell silent, his words dying in his throat as he took in Murdo's white face and distressed expression. For a moment, they just stared at one another, and David wanted to ask what made Murdo look so stricken, but somehow the words were unutterable.

At last Murdo said quietly, "My father has one of the largest stocks of sheep in the highlands. Most of the people that lived at Kilbeigh when I was a boy were cleared off the land a decade ago." He paused, then added, "Two villages were burned down altogether."

When he was finished, he looked calm, but a muscle leapt in his cheek, betraying his tension.

David didn't know what to say. He searched Murdo's face, looking for some clue as to how the man felt about what had happened on his father's lands but he seemed to have control of himself now and there was nothing to see but that cool, impassive expression the man so often wore.

Murdo turned away, heading for the door. "Come on. I've ordered some supper for us. We don't have to leave for the ball for a while yet."

"Supper" consisted of a bewildering array of small, perfectly cooked dishes. Cold roast meats, game terrine, small salad, dressed vegetables. Murdo served a plate out for David, as proper as any footman, and pressed wine upon him. Throughout the meal, he was unfailingly polite, making none of his usual barbed, mocking remarks. David guessed that, for Murdo, perfect manners were probably a sign of displeasure.

David tried to eat, but he had no appetite. He knew, somehow, that his angry words about the clearance of the ordinary highlanders from Murdo's family's lands had touched a nerve, and now he regretted the burst of venom that had prompted him to speak so impulsively without knowing anything of Murdo's circumstances.

After a lengthy silence, Murdo let out a huffed breath.

"Damn it all," he muttered. He set down his wineglass with a sigh, and David looked up, meeting his gaze.

"This isn't what I was hoping for," Murdo said by way of explanation, his tone terse.

David stared at him, taking in the glowering gaze and unhappy expression.

"What were you hoping for?" he asked.

"To talk with you," Murdo replied, the dark flush over his cheekbones showing that this was not an easy admission for him. "To persuade you to come back here with me, after the ball and spend the night again."

David didn't say anything in response to that. But

he watched Murdo steadily and thought, *I want that too.*

It wasn't an especially comfortable realisation. There was a world of difference between enjoying the pleasures Murdo Balfour offered as and when the opportunity arose and actively admitting that was what he wanted. Planning to do it in advance and going out of his way to make sure it happened.

"Most of all," Murdo said in a husky voice, "I want you in my bed again."

David swallowed, and he knew that Murdo noticed his reaction.

"This is unwise," David said weakly.

"Is it? How can it be unwise to see the chance of pleasure and to take it?" Murdo replied. "Surely that is the very opposite of being unwise?"

David felt a brief rush of impatience at Murdo's deliberate blindness. "You know why. There are consequences. Pleasure has a price."

"You're talking about regret, and I've told you before, I have no time for regret. I don't believe in it."

"Well, perhaps I do."

Murdo leaned over the table and grasped David's forearm. "Do you regret any of the time you've spent with me, David? Would you undo it if you could? Because let me tell you this, I would not lose a second of it." He paused for a long moment, his dark gaze boring into David, then added, "Why do you think I came back to Edinburgh in the first place?"

David returned Murdo's gaze, arrested by what he saw there, held in place by the hard hand on his arm.

"You came for the King's visit," he said at last. "Your father—"

"My father asked me to come to Edinburgh and nearly fell off his chair when I agreed," Murdo interrupted with grim amusement. "I know for a fact he had at least two different blackmail ideas to use against me when I refused him, as I usually do."

"I don't understand."

"I think you do," Murdo said gently. "But let me make it plain so there's no misunderstanding: what we shared two years ago wasn't enough for me. What we've had this time isn't enough either. I want more."

Well, that was plain. Plain as could be.

David sighed. "You know that, at some point, this has to end."

Murdo's grip on David's arm loosened. "Yes, I know. Just—not now. Let's just allow this to run its course this time."

Run its course? Murdo spoke about this thing between them like it was a fever, an infection that just needed to rage for a while before it inevitably burnt out. He didn't seem to share David's fears at all—that it was more like a maiming. More like lining up to voluntarily have a limb removed that you'd never get back.

"Tell me," Murdo said. "Will you come back here with me tonight, David? Will you come to my bed again?"

And somehow, despite everything, David didn't hesitate. He couldn't have refused the man had his life depended on it.

"Yes," he said. "I will."

To hell with the consequences.

Chapter Twelve

Given how close Murdo's house was to the Assembly Rooms, they walked there, Murdo garnering a good many whistles and teasing catcalls for his highland dress on the way.

The crowds were dense, the carriages and sedan chairs carrying guests to the ball barely able to move. Even on foot it was taking Murdo and David an absurdly long time to make their way to the entrance.

"This could grow ugly," David said as a sedan chair wielded by yelling highlanders charged past, its long poles striking anyone who didn't get out of the way quickly enough. A barrage of profanity was yelled after it by aggrieved members of the crowd.

"I know what you mean," Murdo muttered. "Those lunatics will start a riot behaving like that. Come on, let's get inside and away from this madness."

Murdo took the lead, elbowing his way more roughly through the last bit of crowd that stood between them and the doors to the Assembly Rooms, and David followed in his wake.

The entrance was beautifully decorated. Diaphanous fabric was wound around the columns and arches, and gas-lit transparencies were cleverly placed to create a winding path from the portico to the inner doors, the colourful, shivering images oddly lifelike in the faint breeze.

"Come on," Murdo said in David's ear, his deep voice amused, and David realised he'd come to a standstill halfway through the magical little grotto, staring at the wonders around him like the country bumpkin he was.

"Sorry," he muttered and moved forward, Murdo at his elbow.

They barely got two feet beyond the inner doors before their way was barred by a pair of redcoats brandishing bayonets. Murdo fished a pair of tickets out of his inside pocket and flashed them at the pair. One of the redcoats raised his bayonet, but the other looked unsure.

"This one ain't dressed right," he said to the other. "We're not supposed to let 'em in if they ain't dressed right."

The other one eyed Murdo nervously. "Beggin' your pardon, sir, but Private Jackson 'ere is right. We ain't supposed to let anyone in that ain't in court dress. Or a skirt, of course, like your very good self."

"A *skirt*," Murdo repeated, looking at the man who swallowed conspicuously. "A kilt, you mean?"

"Yes, sir."

"It's not 'sir'," Murdo corrected calmly. "It's 'my lord'. Lord Murdo Balfour, to be precise."

The poor man looked positively nauseated. "Sorry," he said, adding after a painful pause, "my lord."

Murdo let out a long-suffering sigh and turned to David. "Well, Mr. Lauriston, I can only apologise for this ridiculous situation. Would you be good enough to wait here while I go and speak to His Majesty? As his personal guest, I know he will wish you to be admitted, but these fellows apparently have nothing better to do than put us to trouble of asking the King to intervene in the matter personally."

David truly wished he'd worn a bloody kilt now. He was mortified, both on his own behalf and on behalf of the two redcoats who were squirming now.

"Hello there, Murdo! Are my guard dogs giving you jip?"

The new voice came from the bottom of the staircase behind the redcoats, and when David peered round them, it was to see none other than Captain Sinclair walking towards them. He was dressed in a fancier set of the same regimentals his men were wearing, his shako under his arm and a wide smile on his handsome face.

"Ah, Captain," Murdo greeted him. "Apparently, your men aren't satisfied with Mr. Lauriston's dress this evening."

Sinclair chuckled and looked at the redcoat who'd been doing the talking. "Let them through, Jackson. I can vouch for the fact that this gentleman was invited by the King himself."

"Yes, Captain," the man said quickly, and the crossed bayonets were drawn back, clearing their path.

Murdo sailed through the gap, and David followed in his wake.

"No doubt we'll see you later, Captain Sinclair," Murdo said as they passed him.

"No doubt," the captain replied with a roguish grin. "Once the guests are all arrived, we'll shut these doors, and then I fully intend to monopolise all the prettiest ladies. Consider yourselves warned, gentlemen."

Murdo laughed by way of answer, and then they were mounting the magnificent staircase that led to the principal ballroom and the throng of richly dressed guests.

The ballroom had been transformed into the King's own personal throne room. Panels of rich blue velvet were pinned over the windows, their gold-fringed edges brushing the highly polished floor. Massive chandeliers blazed with a thousand candles. A magnificent dais with a gilded throne and a crimson velvet canopy over it had been set up at one end for the King's sole use. He sat there, surrounded by several of his entourage, watching the dancing with a bored expression.

The guests all seemed to be trying to invoke the spirit of the noble *Gael*. How many eagles, David wondered, had died to bedeck the caps and hair ornaments of the ladies and gentlemen at this night's ball? He'd be surprised if there were any birds left in the sky. The quantity and variety of tartan was even more overwhelming: kilts and trousers for the men, shawls and sashes for the ladies. And then there was the sparkle of aristocratic jewellery. Jewels on fingers and wrists and necks; jewels twinkling in cravat folds and on earlobes. The showy dazzle of the rich and titled.

In the open gallery above the ballroom, a small orchestra played refined versions of traditional Scottish airs, suitable only for the slowest and stateliest of dancing. The tone was distinctly sentimental. It was more of the same carefully manufactured patriotism that had overtaken the city over the last few weeks.

"You should pay your respects to the King before we do anything else," Murdo said. "Come along."

Reluctantly, David followed him, coming to a halt at the foot of the King's dais. He did his best to copy Murdo's elegant bow.

"Lord Murdo!" the King exclaimed with evident pleasure. "There you are."

"Good evening, Your Majesty. May I present Mr. Lauriston to you again?"

The King turned his attention to David, his expression going from confusion to understanding in a moment. "Ah, Mr. Lauriston," he said in a jovial way. "My protector from the other day. I was grateful to you, sir."

"Thank you, Your Majesty."

"And are you enjoying the ball? It is magnificent, is it not?"

"Yes, Your Majesty. Quite magnificent."

"Make sure he dances, Lord Murdo," the King said, addressing Murdo now.

"I will," Murdo assured him, and then the King nodded, turning his attention back to the man who sat on his right. That signalled their dismissal, apparently, and a moment later, they were walking away.

"That wasn't too bad, was it?" Murdo said. "And now that your duty's done, you can do as you please."

David smiled. "I suppose so."

"What now, then?" Murdo asked. "Dancing? Something to eat or drink?"

David had already scanned the crowd, seeking Elizabeth, but there was no sign of her in here. "I don't much like dancing," he admitted. "And we've only just had supper. I wouldn't mind a stroll around, but you don't need to nursemaid me. I'm perfectly capable of amusing myself."

"And I'm perfectly happy to accompany you," Murdo replied. "A stroll sounds ideal. Lead on."

So David did, setting off at a slow pace and carefully searching out every alcove and corner with his gaze as they walked, watchful for any sign of Elizabeth. While they walked, Murdo amused him with insightful and sometimes wickedly funny comments about the entertainments and general absurdity of their fellow guests.

"Ah, now, do you see that man standing up there?" Murdo murmured in his ear as they approached the top of another staircase. David glanced in the direction of Murdo's subtle nod, noting a heavy-set older man in a blue coat and red waistcoat standing with his back to the wall, watching people come and go past him. He was the only man present, other than David, sporting neither court nor highland dress, and he wasn't behaving like a guest.

"Who is he?"

"John Townsend," Murdo replied, "a Bow Street runner and a great favourite of the King. He came up here with a few other runners. They're keeping an eye out for known troublemakers, I'm told."

Just then the man's colourless gaze landed on them, lingering a moment as though weighing them up before he glanced away. David shivered, perturbed for some reason by the man's flat, emotionless expression.

"Troublemakers? Here?" he scoffed once they'd moved past, injecting humour into his voice to mask his sudden disquiet.

"You'd be surprised," Murdo replied. "Why do you

think it takes so long for the King to arrive anywhere? Every nook and cranny is checked and double-checked before he so much as sets foot anywhere. He brought his own personal guards as well as the runners, and besides that, there are half a dozen undercover agents circulating wherever he goes—and those are only the ones I know about. I'm quite sure there are others, not to mention the official troops stationed around."

"There are undercover agents circulating here? Tonight?"

"Of course. There are plenty of men who would like to see the King dead. He's hardly the beloved monarch of the people."

"You think not?" David asked dryly, gesturing around him.

Murdo gave a soft laugh. "Yes, it's odd, isn't it? He's proving to be bizarrely popular up here. Who'd've thought it?"

Who indeed, but it was true. The sudden and unexpected public affection for the King in Scotland was nothing short of extraordinary. The general populace appeared to have swallowed whole Sir Walter's frankly bizarre invention of the King as some kind of highland Chief of Chiefs, despite his Teutonic ancestry.

David glanced at Murdo, ready to share that observation, but lost his train of thought when their gazes met. Murdo wore that smile that sometimes graced his face, a curving, irrepressible thing with a deep dimple denting the cheek above and a merry sparkle in his dark gaze. What a thing that smile was. Rare and coaxing. David couldn't help but return it, his own mouth curving up in answer, his thoughts quite deserting him for a moment.

"Mr. Lauriston?"

The soft, female voice stopped his thoughts short. He turned to find its owner, his mind supplying a name before he even saw her.

Elizabeth. Standing in the shadows, a slight, apologetic figure.

"Lady Kinnell. How nice to see you—" he began. She stepped forward to meet him, her gaze darting from side to side even as she did so, checking, checking.

She looked fresh and rather lovely in a simple muslin gown with a broad tartan sash fastened at her shoulder by a silver-and-amethyst stag's head brooch. Her expression was wary, though. Careful.

"I saw you earlier," she confided all in a rush, "and I so wanted to speak with you that I came running up here after you! I'm with Alasdair, you see, and he doesn't like me talking to—" Abruptly, she broke off, flushing, plainly not sure how to finish that sentence.

David closed the gap between them, moving closer to her. "I need to speak with you too," he said without preamble. "I have something important to talk to you about. Your father—"

But her gaze was already off him and looking over his shoulder.

"Lord Murdo?" she whispered, sounding faintly horrified.

David turned to see Murdo stepping closer. A stiff, social smile had replaced the rare, genuine one he'd worn a few moments ago.

"How nice to see you, Miss Chalmers," he said in his deep, anglified voice, bowing over her hand. "Or rather, Lady Kinnell. Mr. Lauriston told me of your marriage." He paused, then added, "Congratulations."

She flinched, a barely perceptible twitch, but it was there for an instant before she pasted on a social mask. "Thank you," she said quietly.

She glanced at David again, and he saw a hint of despair there, one that seemed to intensify a moment later for reasons he didn't understand, till a clipped voice behind him said, "Elizabeth, there you are. I've been looking for you."

David and Murdo turned together to face the newcomer, a tall, lean man with a harshly handsome face and prematurely grey hair. David didn't need to be introduced to realise that this was Elizabeth's husband. The familiarity of the man's words and the way Elizabeth looked suddenly guilty told him everything he needed to know.

Kinnell stared down at Elizabeth, his expression unreadable, and she looked down at the floor, avoiding eye contact.

"Good evening, Kinnell." Murdo's greeting drew the man's attention away from Elizabeth. "I wasn't aware you were in town. Up for the celebrations, are you?"

Kinnell looked coolly surprised to be thus addressed, and David wondered if the two men were generally on speaking terms. "Yes," he said. "As are you, I presume?"

"Indeed. This is my charge for the evening, Mr. Lauriston. Mr. Lauriston, Sir Alasdair Kinnell."

David bowed stiffly, and Kinnell favoured him with a nod. "Your charge?"

"Mr. Lauriston made a favourable impression on the King earlier this week. He was personally invited to this evening's ball. I was given the job of making sure Mr. Lauriston appeared." Murdo chuckled. "He is not a man for idle entertainments, are you, Lauriston?"

David wondered what Murdo was about even as he murmured his agreement. "Not generally, no."

"So you see," Murdo interrupted, "when we passed your lady wife, whom I had the great pleasure of meeting two years ago—it was two years, was it not, Lady Kinnell?"—Elizabeth cleared her throat and said she believed it was—"I asked if she would do my friend here the very great honour of dancing with him, as I'm sure no one would be better placed to show him that dancing is not as terrifying as he believes."

David knew then that Murdo understood he needed to talk to Elizabeth and that he needed to get her away from her husband to do that.

And of course, Murdo knew Kinnell of old. Knew he was a bully and brute.

Kinnell frowned and opened his mouth to speak, but Murdo interjected before he could say a word. "I know, it is the height of rudeness to opportune a married lady so shamelessly in the corridor, but I could not help myself. I believe I have had my head turned by the magnificence of the evening." He gave a laugh and slapped Kinnell on the shoulder, then turned to Elizabeth. "I am sorry, my lady, for putting you on the spot. It was ungentlemanly. I have a feeling you were about to refuse me but could not think of a polite way to do it."

Elizabeth looked helplessly at her husband. He didn't so much as glance at her but gave a tight sort of smile. "I am sure Elizabeth would not think of refusing. She would be delighted to dance with your charge, wouldn't you, my dear?"

Elizabeth paused, watching him, wary. Then, barely above a whisper, she said, "Of course. Delighted."

"Good!" Murdo said. "Escort Lady Kinnell to the ballroom, then, Lauriston. Off you go." He turned his shoulder on David and Elizabeth and moved closer to Kinnell, a sheepdog isolating a ram. "My thanks," David heard him murmur in Kinnell's ear. "He's a nice enough fellow, to be sure, but rather dull. Now, I have something I particularly wanted to ask you about, Kinnell. An investment opportunity…"

Chapter Thirteen

David led Elizabeth back to the principal ballroom, where the music was more genteel and the dancing less boisterous. There was already a country dance in full flow, which gave them a respectable reason for strolling around the ballroom instead of joining in.

Elizabeth checked over her shoulder more than once before she glanced at David and said softly, "I am not sure what to make of Lord Murdo."

"What do you mean?"

"The way he distracted Alasdair." She flushed as she admitted what they both already knew—that they had silently colluded, the three of them, so that David and Elizabeth could have a few brief minutes of privacy.

"In truth, I am not sure what to make of him either," David replied. "He had no idea I wished to speak with you, other than by hearing what we said to one another before your husband arrived. But he must have concluded that it was important it should happen."

"Why would he do that?"

David paused briefly. "He knows Kinnell. They were at school together." He watched carefully for her reaction, noting that she flushed more deeply and looked away.

"He pretended you and I didn't know one another. And that story about the King—"

"Actually that part is true. The King did invite me, and Lord Murdo was indeed asked to be my guide this evening."

"But he pretended he didn't know you either."

David paused again. "Well, we do not know each other very well."

"Well enough that he tells lies to help you."

He ignored that observation. "Why did you seek me out, Elizabeth?"

She said nothing about his sudden, uninvited use of her Christian name, just looked at him with eyes that brimmed with unspoken misery.

"I don't know," she said. "I wanted to speak to someone familiar, I suppose. Someone from my old life. I'm worried about Father too. I wanted to talk about him with someone who knows him. Since I married, I've barely seen him, or my sisters."

"He's worried about you too," David replied. "He asked me to watch out for you."

"Did he?" she whispered. "Why?"

Their time together would be short. David did not have the luxury of tact tonight.

"He's not well. And he believes you are unhappy, that you have been so since your marriage."

Sudden tears welled in her eyes.

"Is it true?" David asked. "Is he right to be worried?"

The silence seemed to stretch unbearably until, at last, she whispered, "Yes. But what can I do?"

David felt sick. Somehow he had imagined she would not want to admit that she was being mistreated, that she would paste a bright smile on her face and tell him that everything was all right. Her admission about her position and her palpable fear undid him.

He placed his hand on top of her own where it rested on his sleeve. "Does he hurt you?" he asked quietly.

She didn't look at him, but she nodded. "I hate him," she whispered. "He is—cruel. I regret marrying him every single day. I didn't know what manner of man he was."

"I was surprised when I heard the news. You barely knew him before you were engaged."

She gave a bitter laugh. "I was a fool," she said. "I thought I cared for nothing anymore. I thought I was heartbroken and it didn't matter who I married if I couldn't have the man I wanted."

David's heart sank. She was speaking about him,

he realised.

"I have no intention of taking a wife, Miss Chalmers."

"I'm so sorr—"

"Please don't apologise," she interrupted. "It was dramatic and self-indulgent of me to throw myself away like that. Plenty of people warned me against marrying so hastily." She gave another bitter laugh at that. "But I wouldn't listen."

David's gut clenched. Even now, he had no real idea what Kinnell was capable of, but Elizabeth's grim expression was telling him more than he wanted to know. And after this dance, David would have to deliver her back to the man. It was a thought that made his stomach churn with impotent anger.

"Do you remember my friend, Mr. MacLennan?" he asked now. "You met him the other day—"

"Yes, of course. He asked me if Alasdair had hurt me. I couldn't believe his nerve." She laughed, but it was a low, desperate noise.

"Euan is an unusual man."

"And a radical," she said bluntly.

"Yes," David agreed gently. "He is a radical. He believes in equality, between the classes, and between men and women, amongst other things."

"He told me that. He said—he said I should run away from Alasdair."

David saw her pale throat bob as she swallowed.

"Do you want to?"

Her eyes flickered from side to side, fearful. "He will never let me go."

"Do you want to leave?" David persisted.

"*Yes!*"

How could a mere whisper hold so much yearning? So much yearning and so little hope.

David tightened his hold on her hand. "Listen to me, then. Euan and I are both willing to help you. But your husband has rights over you. It would not be easily done."

"I know."

"So you would have to be willing to run away—far away—with nothing but the clothes you stand up in. To trust Euan to get you to London, where you can start a new life." He paused. "You have to decide if your life with Kinnell is so bad as to be worth that kind of sacrifice."

"It is," she said, without hesitation. "But, my family... David, I don't want to shame them!"

David shook his head. "Your father is already concerned about you, and—you must have realised this already—he is not well. I think it would comfort him to know you were away from Kinnell. I think he would make financial arrangements for you, if you asked him, or if I did so on your behalf."

She looked suddenly afraid. Afraid to hope, perhaps.

"It would have to be soon," she said. "We are due

to leave for Galloway in just over a week's time, and I do not want to go back there. I can't go back there." She shuddered as though at some unpleasant memory, and David's stomach clenched again. He never wanted to learn what put that fear into her eyes.

"When are you alone?"

She sent him a despairing look. "Never. Alasdair is always there, or a servant. I am not allowed out without one of the footmen. When I came to your rooms with Catherine, it was the first time I'd been out without a servant in months, and that was only because, when I got to Catherine's house, Donald told my footman, Fraser, to go to the kitchen while we had tea. Then Donald ordered the carriage to be brought round, and we left without him. It was Donald's doing—he didn't even think to fetch Fraser—but Alasdair turned Fraser off without a reference when we got back." She paused. Swallowed again. "And I was punished."

Her expression was haunted as she remembered whatever her punishment had been.

The music of the dance ended just then, and the dancers began to rearrange, some leaving the floor and others joining new sets.

"We should dance," Elizabeth said. "If Alasdair comes in and we are strolling and talking, he will be angry."

"Come on, then," David said, turning around and

leading her towards the nearest incomplete set. "We have another few minutes before you have to go back to him."

"We are not going to be able to talk anymore," she said, her voice breaking. "If I cannot even speak to you, how am I ever to get away from him?"

David squeezed her hand. "We will be able speak a little," he said. "We will make a plan."

The dance was a sedate one, with gentle passes and turns, light skipping and stately promenades. David questioned her about the rhythms of her household whenever they encountered one another in the dance. He asked her too about the events that she and Kinnell would be attending during the last week of the King's visit.

Towards the end of the dance, on one of their passes, David felt Elizabeth stiffen. He followed her gaze and found Kinnell and Murdo standing together at the end of the dance floor, watching them.

"He's back," Elizabeth said despairingly.

David turned to her, as the dance demanded, and looked into her eyes. "Listen to me," he said. "This is what we are going to do. You're going to the theatre on Tuesday, aren't you? You must be ready to leave then, that very night, in the clothes you are wearing. I will speak with your father about money for you. I will also speak to Euan about arrangements for getting you to London. Are you willing to travel with him to a safe place?"

The dance parted them. They turned away from each other to stroll down parallel lines of the set, coming to face one another once more at the end.

"If you trust Mr. MacLennan, I will trust him too," she said.

Did he? Did he trust Euan MacLennan?

He thought of his history with Euan. Two years ago, Euan had held him at gunpoint and threatened to put a bullet in him. But he hadn't done it—and his every action had been for his brother and his beliefs. There was no greed in Euan, no selfishness. He was passionate and idealistic. Impetuous and perhaps somewhat naïve, but a good man.

"A man will fight for hate for a long time, but he will fight for love to the death."

"I would trust him with my life," David said simply. He'd done it once before.

"Then I will trust him too," she whispered as she curtsied to him, ending their dance. "And I will be ready on Tuesday, at the theatre. What time will it happen?"

David bowed to her, thinking quickly. "Half past nine," he said. The play would be well underway by then. "Get away from Kinnell, however you can. And make your way to the front door. I will try to get a ticket so I can meet you inside, but even if I cannot, I *will* find you. I promise."

"Half past nine," she said. "Pray, do not fail me."

CHAPTER FOURTEEN

"I hope it was worth it," Murdo said under his breath as Kinnell escorted Elizabeth away, his hand at the small of her back. "I fear she may pay for this, later."

David glanced quickly at the other man. "Why do you say that?"

"Did you notice how angry he was when he found her talking to us? I don't think my attempt to take the blame cut the mustard with him somehow."

"I thought he believed you," David replied. "You were quite convincing."

"Oh, I think he believed me, but he'll be angry with her anyway. He doesn't want her talking to anyone on her own, does he?"

David pondered that acute observation with a sick feeling. He had a feeling Murdo was right, and he didn't want to think of what Elizabeth might be facing when she got home tonight.

"I shouldn't have interfered," Murdo said flatly. "It was impulsive. I didn't think—"

"I'm glad you did," David interrupted, adding after a pause, "though I'm still puzzled as to *why* you did it."

Murdo frowned. "It was her face when she said she wanted to speak to you. She looked desperate." He paused, then added softly, "I think she still loves you."

"She doesn't love me," David protested. He meant to defend her, but somehow the words felt like a betrayal, and fresh guilt bloomed in him. Elizabeth *had* loved him once, even if she had every reason to hate him now. "She is unhappy," he added. "She needed to speak to me about her father. And I had—things to tell her from him."

"You are blind, David," Murdo said, though he smiled faintly. "If you'd seen the expression on her face..."

"I *did* see it," David retorted. "And she is not heart-sore over me, I assure you. Not anymore. Though she is heart-sore, and for good reason."

"I hope she's all right tonight," Murdo said. "I would not wish Kinnell's anger on a dog, never mind a gentle young woman."

"She's stronger than she looks," David replied. He said it with more firmness than he felt, then forced himself to change the subject before he revealed more than he ought to. "Tell me, how much longer must we stay here before our departure would be commented upon? Have we put in enough of an appearance, do you think?"

Murdo raised his brows, surprised. "We've barely been here an hour and a half."

David shrugged. "Isn't that enough? I've danced, and I've paid my respects to the King. Do you want to stay?"

"Not particularly," Murdo admitted, a small smile just touching his lips. "Do you want to leave right this minute?"

"Why not? I am not much of one for dancing, as you know."

Murdo laughed at that, a warm chuckle that made David smile. "Would you care, perhaps, for a nip of brandy by a warm fire instead?" The look he gave David suggested that sitting by a warm fire was very far from what he really had in mind.

"That sounds very pleasant," David agreed, grinning back.

They made their way downstairs, passing Townsend the runner again as they went. He observed their departure with the same bland watchfulness as before, and David felt oddly guilty as they passed him, as though the man knew precisely what they were up to.

Soon enough they were strolling through the little grotto of lights and emerging from the outer doors into a sea of people and noise.

The crowd was even denser and rowdier than before. A line of soldiers had been deployed to guard the entrance to the Assembly Rooms with raised bayonets.

One of them stood aside to let David and Murdo pass through, then just as quickly took his post again.

"Let's go," Murdo muttered in David's ear. "I don't like this crowd."

David nodded his agreement. "I'll follow you."

Murdo began to push his way through the tightly packed throng, and David plunged after him, staying as close as possible. They attracted a few curses, though thankfully nothing worse, as they fought the tide of people. Everyone seemed to be trying to get nearer to the entrance to the ball, possibly hoping to see the King when he emerged later.

After a quarter hour of jostling and squeezing, they were through the worst of it and striding down the hill to Murdo's house.

"Need I ask if you enjoyed yourself?" Murdo asked, his tone very dry.

"Let's just say I'm glad it's over."

Murdo chuckled. "I was surprised you came at all. You're not generally one to do anything you don't want to, even at the request of a king."

"It was interesting," David prevaricated, unable to disclose that he'd come to see Elizabeth and for no other reason. Well, perhaps for one other reason…

"Interesting, how?"

"The pageantry of it all. It might have been of dubious authenticity, but it was magnificently done, I have to admit."

"Ah, we're back to this, are we? Your disapproval of all the tartan flummery?"

"I'm not being disapproving. It's just that my idea of Scotland is not the same as the one that's being portrayed to the King, that's all."

"What is yours, then?"

"Mine?"

"Yes, yours. What is David Lauriston's Scotland like?"

"Well—this is the Scotland I inhabit now, I suppose." David gestured around them, at the elegant New Town with its clean lines and gas lamps and private gardens. "Rational. Modern. Just think—who lives in these houses?"

"I do, for one," Murdo said, his white teeth gleaming as he flashed a grin at David.

"True, but most of them are occupied by merchants, lawyers, bankers. Professional men. Sir Walter might like to promote the fantasy of noble highland chiefs, but these are the men of the new Scotland. And they don't look to aristocrats to guide them. They're more interested in what Adam Smith and David Hume would have had to say."

Murdo snorted. "It sounds to me like you're swapping one kind of privilege for another. Does it really matter whether our kingmakers are aristocrats or philosophers or bankers?"

"Ah, but this is only the beginning," David retorted. "One day we will have universal suffrage. And then, how things will change!"

Murdo merely shrugged. "We'll see. I have always found that men are defined more by their desire to do each other down rather than to lift each other up, but time will tell."

"You are a pessimist," David accused, smiling. "I think we are better than that."

"I'm not so sure," Murdo replied. "And I'm not sure the general population want the changes you think they do."

"Oh, they want them. That crowd in George Street might've started out cheering, but there was an angry undercurrent there. You felt it as well as I did."

"There was something, yes. But haven't crowds always been like that? It's the mob. A mob is capable of things individuals are not."

Murdo came to a halt, and David stopped beside him, only realising when he looked over the other man's shoulder that they'd reached Murdo's townhouse already.

"So. Here we are again," David said. Despite the serious tone of their conversation, a smile tugged at his lips. He felt like there was laughter inside him, just waiting to escape. He knew, without the benefit of a looking glass, that he looked happy—he saw his elation reflected on Murdo's face, in the curving smile that mirrored his own.

"Shall we go inside?" Murdo asked, one eyebrow raised.

David grinned, and then they were dashing up the steps together like boys, practically bowling over the footman who opened the glossy door.

Murdo briefly assumed a more sober expression in front of his servant, issuing a few brief orders as they handed off their outer garments—primarily that no one should intrude upon their privacy without being called for—and then they were mounting the stairs to Murdo's chambers.

They maintained their composure right up to the door of Murdo's sitting room, but the moment they stepped inside and the door closed behind them, they came together in a hard embrace, their mouths fusing in a deep, hot kiss.

"Ah, Christ but I need this—" Murdo gasped when they broke apart. He pressed his mouth to David's throat, his hands working to strip away David's cravat and expose the tender flesh beneath. The scrape of his roughened cheek and the sharp nip of his teeth made David hunch a shoulder in startled pleasure, a prickle of gooseflesh rising up the back of his neck.

David's cock felt as hard as a hammer, his balls tight and aching. A twitchy desire for Murdo to touch his arse consumed him, shaming him even as he yearned. Over the last few nights, he'd fallen asleep reliving what it felt like to have Murdo's mouth teasing the entrance to his body, the terrifying, wonderful feeling of Murdo's fingers penetrating him.

Just the thought of that now, right at the moment that Murdo nipped his throat again, made David groan and circle his hips against Murdo's, their clothed cocks brushing as he did so.

"What do you want?" David breathed against Murdo's ear. "Tell me."

Tell me you want to fuck me.

"I hardly know," Murdo murmured against David's skin. "Everything. You. I can't get enough of you."

David shifted, frustrated, unwilling to ask for what he wanted even as he craved it.

Murdo raised his head, perhaps sensing David's turmoil. He looked down at David with an unreadable expression for what felt like the longest moment, and David stared back, trying to interpret his look, willing him to speak.

At last Murdo said, startling him, "Is it that you want to fuck *me*? We've never spoken about that possibility, have we? I admit, I've avoided the subject."

David just stared at him, astonished into silence. In truth, he'd never considered that possibility, and now he found himself wondering why.

"I don't know," he said at last, adding after a pause, "Why? Would you let me?"

Murdo was silent for a long moment. "I'd be willing to try." His voice was calm, but a muscle leapt in his cheek, a betraying tic. "The truth is, I've not allowed anyone to do that to me for a long time. Not since that first time I told you about. The thought of letting anyone—" He gave an awkward laugh in lieu of finishing the sentence, then added, "But I'd try—for you."

David felt the oddest easing inside his chest, a ligature being loosened, a constriction he hadn't even known was there, giving way. He raised a hand and stroked the cheek where that tic had leapt.

"I don't think we should do that tonight," he said. "The truth is, I wouldn't have the first idea what to do. We should do it the other way first, I think."

"The other way?"

"You fucking me. At least you know what to do." David tried to look nonchalant, but he knew that the heat he felt creeping into his cheeks had to be turning his pale skin scarlet.

Murdo was silent for a long moment. "You're sure?"

"Yes."

"I don't want you to feel pushed into it."

"I don't. I want it. I want you."

Murdo's dark gaze searched his own, as though checking for uncertainty. "All right. I'll do everything I can to make it good."

"I know."

I know you'll try.

"Come on, then. If we're doing this, we're doing it properly, in my bed."

Murdo took David's hand and towed him into the bedchamber, leaving him stranded in the middle of the room for a moment while he lit a branch of candles off the fire. After placing the candles on the mantelpiece, he turned his attention to the big bed, stripping the silken bedcovers entirely away to reveal the bone-white linen sheets below, a stark field for their play. Then he returned to face David and pulled him into another deep kiss.

"I don't even know why I want this so much," he breathed against David's mouth when he released his lips. "I've had plenty of lovers I've never fucked. I don't even think it's the physical thing I want so much as—"

"As what?" David's lips grazed Murdo's as he spoke, and just that brief, brushing caress made Murdo groan and press their mouths together again, and whatever they'd been talking about was purely lost, a half-formed thought that fell away as their kiss deepened.

Murdo began to strip the clothes from David's body with the skill of man who'd undertaken the task many times before, his fingers nimble and knowing. Once David was naked, he urged him to lie down on the mattress of the big bed. The linen was cool under David's naked back, the candlelight casting a warm, dim glow over his skin. Murdo paused a moment to look at him, his gaze eating up the picture David presented, lingering on the hard, aching shaft that rose from the brush of fox-red hair between David's legs.

Murdo stripped away his own clothes with no care for their expensive elegance, tossing them aside like rags, his turbulent gaze intent on David. And Christ, but he was a sight to behold. Tall and powerful and dark. He was no fop, this Lord Murdo Balfour.

Fully naked now, Murdo crossed the room to open a drawer in the armoire and withdraw something. As he turned back to the bed, David saw that he held a small bottle, stoppered with a cork and three-quarters full of something greenish-gold and viscous.

"What's that?" David asked.

"Oil. It makes it easier." Murdo crawled onto the mattress and straddled David's thighs. His gaze was hot, his faint smile promising. "I'm going to rub it on you—and in you—and do other unspeakable things to you too." He grinned, boyishly handsome, carelessly happy. "Things that will have you so ready for me you'll be begging for my cock."

David gave a nervous laugh. Was it possible he'd beg? Given how anxious he felt about what was to come, it seemed unlikely.

Something about his thoughts must've shown on his face. A tiny frown appeared between Murdo's dark brows.

"We don't have to do this—" he began.

"I want to," David interrupted, his voice firm.

Murdo stared at him for a long moment; then he nodded. "All right, but I'll stop anytime you want. Just say the word if you change your mind."

"I will," David murmured back. "If I want you to."

Murdo tossed the bottle of oil onto the mattress—it landed a foot away from David's hip, within easy reaching distance—and dropped down to cover David's body with his own. He was heavy and warm, and the faint roughness of his chest hair teased David's skin. His scent, deliciously male, carried the hint of a dozen aromas, the clean tang of his sweat, wine and woodsmoke, a hint of bitter orange from the pomade he'd dressed his hair with.

David breathed in, arching his back and pulling Murdo closer.

"Do we have all night?" Murdo breathed in his ear. "Will you stay till morning?"

"Yes."

They'd have the whole night, and maybe part of the morning too. The hours ahead spooled out like ribbon, endless-seeming.

"Good," Murdo said. "Then I can take my time."

He began by exploring the hollows of David's throat with his mouth, moving slowly down, over sternum, nipples and flanks. He traced the deep crescents of David's lower ribs and dipped his tongue into the shallow indentation of his navel.

His exploration was tender and slow, and it brought David more than mere pleasure. The touch of Murdo's mouth made him feel alive, his neglected body given meaning by the attentive desire of his lover. Each kiss saying, *you are here, in this world, with me.*

Murdo moved farther down, his soft kiss following the line of David's hipbone to the deep furrow between thigh and groin. Shifting position, he gently pushed David's thighs apart, settling himself into the space he made, his big body moving with unexpected grace.

It occurred to David, distantly, that he should be embarrassed to be opened up like this, Murdo's broad palms firm against his thighs, holding him ruthlessly open. But he felt no shame as Murdo looked him over, then finally, achingly slowly, dipped his head again.

David gasped at the sensation of Murdo's mouth on the tender skin of his inner thigh, growing restless as Murdo continued his languid journey, his attention oblique and maddening. Murdo's agile tongue skirted David's hard cock, the prickly sac of his scrotum, his aching hole, concentrating on the less direct but still sensitive areas around them, and David shifted under his attentions, moaning, his hips bucking up in frustration.

"God, Murdo—" he exclaimed, his voice husky with need. "Fuck me, please!"

Murdo laughed softly, raising himself to his knees between David's spread thighs to look down at him, his ready smile bright with mischief and pleasure. David's breath caught in his throat as their gazes met, and for a moment, Murdo's expression turned oddly serious, the merry glint in his dark eyes briefly softening into something infinitely more tender and affectionate. Then desire took over again, and he reached for David's nipples, thumbing the tiny peaks before running his hands down David's flanks with a low moan.

By now, the sharp nerves David had battled at the start of this had dimmed to little more than a background murmur. Now his body yearned for the attention it had feared, remembering the pleasure Murdo's fingers had given him once before.

Murdo took hold of David's hips, pulling him closer and simultaneously pushing his legs back. David's pelvis tilted till his knees were almost touching his chest.

"Hold your legs up for me," Murdo murmured, and David complied, grasping the backs of his thighs.

Shame seemed to have deserted him, and he could only watch, breathless, as Murdo reached for the bottle that lolled next to David's hip, unstoppering the cork with his teeth.

Murdo poured a thin stream of the glistening oil over David's groin. The viscous liquid slid over him, warm and slow, like honey. It trickled down his scrotum, past the soft patch of skin below his sac and farther still, right down into the tender groove that led to the entrance to his body. The oil slid slowly all the way to his hole, where Murdo caught it with his waiting fingers, gathering it up and spreading it over the tight muscle.

His fingertips were blunt, the slippery oil allowing them to tease the edges of David's hole and dip fleetingly inside, making David twist and moan with the brief pain and deeper pleasure that exploration brought.

Murdo must've tossed the bottle aside, because now his other hand, also slick with the oil, worked David's shaft in counterpoint to those exploring fingers, while David held back his trembling legs. After only a minute or so, David was crying out desperately, half in protest at the prospect of climaxing so soon.

"I'm going to come!" he gasped.

"No, you're not," Murdo replied, easing his hand from David's cock. "You're not going to come till I'm inside you."

That promise alone was nearly enough to finish him off, till Murdo distracted him with a new sensation, his finger entering David's body, then withdrawing and reentering. The slight pain of the first thrust removed the threat of immediate release, but it wasn't long before David was growing used to the sensation, then craving it, his hips moving in time to the thrust of Murdo's hand.

Then there was more, more *heft*. David wasn't sure how many fingers Murdo was using on him but it was more than one, and it felt good. His body was stretching, accommodating Murdo's demands with an ease that astounded the tiny part of his mind that was still able to think.

The pleasure Murdo was giving him now was coming from somewhere deep inside him, somewhere unreachable, yet vital, that he was sure he'd never known about before Murdo. He wanted to tell Murdo that, but when he tried to speak, all that he could get out was, "Murdo—*God*—"

Murdo's fierce, glittering gaze did not waver as he watched David writhe.

"I think I'm going to—please, you have to fuck me—" he begged.

Murdo said nothing, but he withdrew his fingers from David's body and reached for the bottle of oil again, this time letting the greeny-gold stream trickle over his own cock before stoppering the bottle and tossing it aside. He worked the hard, tumescent flesh of his shaft for a few moments, biting his lower lip against the easy pleasure. Then he moved forward, shifting on his knees till his prick was pointed at David's hole.

"Keep your knees pulled back and bear down when I press into you," he said. Then he pushed.

"*Christ!*" David gasped.

The bulbous head of a prick felt very different to a finger—or even a few fingers. Fingers were nimble, flexible. This was brutal and blunt, a battering ram made flesh, and the first sudden stretch was a painful, shocking intrusion.

"Sorry," Murdo hissed. "Just wait—breathe for a while."

David swallowed and did as he was bid, breathing slowly in and out, while Murdo stayed very still, the head of his cock lodged inside David's passage.

After a minute, the pain began to ease, though David still felt alarmingly full.

"All right," he whispered, though his erection had wilted. "You can move now."

"Do you want me to stop?" Murdo gritted out. "I'll stop."

"No. Do it. I'll tell you if I can't go on."

Murdo began to slowly move again, pushing his hips forward in small increments, until at last he was fully seated inside David.

"God, you feel good," Murdo murmured, dropping his forehead to rest against David's. "I never thought—" He broke off, leaving the sentence incomplete, reaching instead for David's wilted shaft to coax him back to hardness. As he worked David's cock with his hand, he pulled back his hips, just a very little, before carefully easing back into David's passage, making the tiny rocking movement a little bigger each time.

Slowly, relentlessly, pleasure began to build again. Slowly, David grew more used to the sensation of Murdo's prick inside his body. And then, after a dozen or so of those careful, searching jabs of his hips, Murdo thrust again, and this time there was a jolt of pure, searing pleasure, as though Murdo had pierced that vital, secret place David had felt earlier deep inside his body. The sensation was so intense it made him gasp and clutch at Murdo's arms.

"*Jesus!*"

Murdo's smile unfurled, secret and delighted. Rare and beautiful.

"There it is," he said.

And then he was drawing out farther and pushing back in, piercing that spot again and again with meticulously accurate thrusts. David twisted and squirmed, unable to control the guttural, begging sounds coming from his aching throat. And then, too soon, too soon his body was surrendering to the inevitability of orgasm. He called out Murdo's name as his climax roared through him, purging him, his seed spattering his belly in helpless pulses.

Seconds later, Murdo was following him. His powerful hands clutched hard at David's hips as his rhythmic movements grew suddenly jerky and graceless, an unholy cry on his lips as he emptied himself inside David's body, then slumped forward to rest his forehead on David's chest.

They lay there, silent, for a long time, damp flesh cooling in the night air. At last, one of the candles guttered out, sending out a thin stream of smoke like a prying finger, and Murdo rose, crossing the room to the armoire where he poured water into a ewer and washed himself briskly.

That taken care of, he dampened a cloth and brought it back to the bed, ignoring the hand David held out for the cloth and sitting down on the mattress to tend to David himself.

With tender swipes, he cleared away the remaining traces of oil and semen, then rescued the bedcovers from the floor and draped them over David's prone body. Finally, he snuffed out the last two candles and joined David in bed again, pushing and prodding till David took the hint and turned onto his side, allowing Murdo to curl his big body around David's back.

David wanted to say something, to acknowledge what had just passed between them, but he couldn't seem to find the words. He thought that Murdo must feel the same. The silence between them felt oddly sacred.

Sleep. He would sleep. Time enough in the morning to talk.

Murdo's soft kiss on the nape of his neck was the last thing he remembered before his dreams took him.

Chapter Fifteen

Saturday, 24th August, 1822

David woke to birdsong, the smell of morning chocolate...and an aching arse.

Opening his eyes, he realised he was alone in bed. The tinkle of cutlery came from the adjoining sitting room, and Murdo's voice, a low murmur.

Another voice. Obsequious, respectful. The door opening, then closing again.

Moments later, Murdo appeared in the doorway to the bedchamber, dressed in a dark blue dressing gown that was as elegantly formal as David's evening clothes.

He smiled at David. "You're awake."

David offered an embarrassed smile in return. "Only just."

"Do you know what time it is?"

David frowned at that, considering. He'd always been an early riser, the ingrained habit of a born-and-bred farm boy, and his sense of time rarely failed him.

"Half past nine," Murdo offered without waiting for an answer.

When David's jaw dropped open with shock, Murdo laughed.

"You're corrupting me," David said, sitting up, then felt his cheeks scorch as he recalled just how much corrupting Murdo had done last night.

Murdo watched him blush, his head to one side. "Do you regret it?" he asked. His tone was careful, those dark eyes watchful.

"No!" David exclaimed, almost offended to be asked. "Not at all!"

Murdo looked perfectly relaxed, lounging in the doorway, yet David detected a minute easing of strain in those broad shoulders at David's vehement protest.

"I wondered if you'd have second thoughts," he admitted.

"No, I'm—" David paused. "I'm glad."

"Good," Murdo said. Then he cleared his throat and turned away. "Why don't you come and have some breakfast, then."

David watched him go before he hopped out of bed to pull on his drawers, shirt and breeches. Thus attired, he wandered into the sitting room. As before, the table was set with snowy linen and fine dishes. Fine food and—yes, his nose hadn't tricked him—there was morning chocolate this time too. David tried the chocolate, but it was too sweet for his taste.

"We drank beer for breakfast, on the farm," he said, setting the chocolate aside and reaching for the teapot. "My father swore by it. Still does."

"Not whisky?" Murdo said casually as he dissected a kipper. "I thought that was your favourite tipple."

At David's silence, he looked up, frowning in a puzzled way. "Sorry," he said. "I was only jesting. And you do drink a fair old lot of whisky, don't you?"

Oddly enough, David thought, he'd been drinking less since Murdo had come back. Even at last night's ball, he'd just sipped at some wine punch. He wasn't sure precisely why that was. Perhaps it was because it was in the evenings when he was alone with his thoughts that he tended to indulge most freely. There had been fewer of those nights lately, and even when he was alone, he'd had other matters taking up his attention.

It was good to wake without a thick head and a thicker tongue. Good to feel clear-headed. Perhaps, when Murdo went back to London, he'd try to lessen his drinking. Except that the thought Murdo would soon be leaving, perhaps never to return, made David feel like doing nothing else so much as sinking a bottle of the hard stuff to the very last dregs.

Ah, perhaps he *should* regret last night after all.

"Did I offend you?" Murdo asked, still frowning. "I didn't mean to."

David made himself look at Murdo, at his worried face. "No, not at all," he said, smiling weakly, and turned his attention back to his coddled eggs, but it was difficult to eat when nausea ate at him, and soon enough he put his cutlery down and placed his napkin on his plate.

"Is that all you're having?" Murdo asked.

"I'm not especially hungry this morning," David replied. "In fact, I should really be going."

It wasn't untrue. He had to go and see Chalmers about Elizabeth, and then he had to discuss arrangements with Euan. He would have to see if he could get a ticket for the Theatre Royal performance too. He had a great deal to do.

And maybe a little distance between him and Murdo would be a good thing.

Murdo sighed. "David, please don't go, I didn't mean—"

"You didn't offend me, truly," David said hurriedly, rising. "But in truth, I have to go."

Murdo rose with him. "Listen, wait a moment. When can I see you again?" He shook his head as soon as the words were out, as though annoyed at himself.

"I don't know," David said, adding after a pause, "And I'm not sure if it's a good idea, to be honest."

Murdo's expression hardened, his lips thinning. "You said you weren't having second thoughts about last night."

"I'm not. I—"

"You said you were *glad*, Goddamn it!"

"I was. I *am*. It's just that…" Was he really going

to say this? "You'll be leaving soon, Murdo. Maybe in a matter of days. And I don't know how I—that is, I don't want to make this any harder than it needs to be—" He broke off, his chest heaving as though he'd run a mile, to discover Murdo staring at him with a stricken look on his face.

Turning on his heel, David stalked into the bedroom and began collecting up his crumpled clothes, pulling them on in jerky movements. Behind him, he heard Murdo's soft footfalls following him into the room, though he said nothing till David turned round, fully dressed.

"It's true that I'll be leaving Edinburgh," Murdo said quietly. "I'm planning to travel up to Perthshire in a week or so, and I'll be there for a while before I go back to London in the new year, but I could drop in on you on my way back down, and I'm usually in Scotland at some point every year—" He broke off, biting his lip before continuing. "I understand your reservations, but I don't want this to end. At the very least, I'd like to see you again before I go to Perthshire."

David stared at him. Murdo might talk about dropping in for brief visits here and there, but the truth was clear to David. If there was any future in this, it was a future in which they would have little more than moments together. Moments strung together with years and years of waiting. If he had any sense, he'd walk away right now and not look back. And yet...last night had been beyond his most vivid imaginings. The thought of having *that* again, just one more time, was damn near irresistible. There would be a reckoning, yes, but it wasn't one he could avoid now anyway. The only question was how much of Murdo he let himself have before that reckoning came.

Before he could say anything, Murdo spoke again.

"Come to the royal performance at the Theatre Royal with me on Tuesday. I've got a whole box to myself, and after, we can come back here for supper. Say yes, David. Please."

Was this fate?

David wasn't a superstitious man, but when something like this happened, you ignored it at your peril. He could see it all now. He would go to the theatre with Murdo, slip out of the box to meet Elizabeth at the designated time, and once he'd seen her safely outside and released her into Euan's care, he would return to Murdo. When the performance was finished, they would go to Murdo's townhouse and have another perfect night together, just like last night. And that would be it between them. When David woke up in the morning, he would say good-bye to Murdo, and that part of his life would be over. The reckoning would come then, of course, but this time he would be ready for it.

"All right," he said carefully. "Tuesday. I'll look forward to it."

David went to see Chalmers straight from Murdo's house.

The footman showed him into Chalmers's study as usual and asked him to wait. Eventually, after twenty minutes, the door opened and Chalmers entered, leaning on the same footman's arm. As before, he wore a dressing gown and looked drawn. David suspected he had been in bed.

"It's good to see you, my boy," Chalmers said.

"You didn't need to get up," David chided him, rising to greet him and guide him into the chair behind his desk.

"It's good for me to get up," Chalmers replied. "Lying in bed all day just makes me feel worse." He turned to the footman. "Prentice, would you fetch a tray of tea?"

The footman bowed and withdrew, leaving them alone.

"So, is this just a courtesy visit, or do you have a purpose?"

"The latter, I'm afraid."

"You're afraid?"

"It concerns Elizabeth."

Chalmers paled. "Something I should know?"

David steeled himself. "I met her last night, at the Peers' Ball. With her husband."

"How was she?" the older man whispered.

"I'll come to that, but I need to ask you something

first," David said. "The last time I came here, you told me you were worried about her," he began. "And you said you were unhappy about her marriage."

"Yes," Chalmers said carefully. "What of it?"

"I need you to tell me, bluntly, why you were so concerned. Was it really just that she seemed more subdued to you, or was there more?"

Chalmers swallowed. "It is difficult to talk about these things, and you—you are not a family member."

"And yet it was me you asked to look out for her," David pointed out gently.

The older man closed his eyes. "Yes."

"Come, then. I know this is not something you would do lightly. So let us talk frankly about Elizabeth's predicament. I think there is more to this than you first said."

When Chalmers opened his eyes, they gleamed with a film of tears. David had never seen the man like this before. Chalmers was a cheerful man, full of bonhomie. Even when he was confined to a sickbed, he joked and laughed, making light of his troubles. But here, today, he looked torn up and ragged with worry.

"I believe he mistreats her," Chalmers said at last, and the admission was heavy with certainty. "I've seen some bruises—and I worry about what I can't see." Chalmers dashed a hand across his wet eyes. "And she is so *silent* in his presence. I think he means to cut us off from her. I looked forward so much to this visit, but I have only seen her twice, once when she came here with him, and once when I forced myself out of bed to go to his house."

David put his hand over the older man's and squeezed, much as he'd done last night to Elizabeth. "You have seen it then," he said, and he was relieved that he would not have to tell Chalmers the worst of it.

"He was married before, you know," Chalmers said. "His first wife died." He looked up, and the expression on his face was distraught.

"I heard that too," David said.

"Tell me what you observed last night."

"I saw that she is afraid of Kinnell," David said quietly. "He did not want to let her out of his sight, but I managed to speak with her alone for a few minutes while we danced." *Thank you, Murdo.* "I could see that a chance to speak with her alone would not come again, so I did not waste time but told her straightaway that you were worried about her and asked if she was happy."

"And what did she say?"

David swallowed, only too aware of how much distress this would cause his mentor. "There is no easy way to say this. She confirmed your fears. She admitted that she is unhappy, and that she is afraid of him. She said that he watches her—or has her watched by servants. Keeps her away from anyone who might try to help her."

Chalmers was chalk white by now, and his hand trembled under David's.

"Does he hurt her?"

David paused. Everything in him wanted to spare Chalmers, but he could not lie. "She did not say much, but I think so, yes. She dreads going back to his estate with him where they will be alone."

"God in heaven, these were my worst fears," Chalmers said, his voice cracking. "What can I do, lad?"

"Listen to me," David said firmly. "Now I will tell you why I am here. And I want you to hear me out, even if your first reaction is to say no."

Chalmers settled a little in response to David's calm manner. "Tell me."

David took a deep breath. "I told Elizabeth I would help her run away from Kinnell, if she wants to."

Chalmers's eyes widened. "What? What did she say?"

"She said yes. She is desperate enough to run from him with no more than the clothes on her back."

"And you think I would not approve?" Chalmers sounded angry.

David let out a sigh of relief. "I wasn't sure. Many parents would say their daughter should stay with her husband, even if she was being mistreated."

Chalmers was silent a moment. "My wife would

probably say so," he admitted. "It's why I asked you to look out for Elizabeth. So that when I'm gone, there will be someone—"

"You are not going anywhere," David interrupted roughly.

"Yes, I am," Chalmers replied quietly. "The physician says it will be a matter of months. Half a year at most, and every day I feel weaker. I am useless to my own daughter in her hour of need. I can only thank God for sending you to us, David."

David tried to disguise the distress that overcame him at Chalmers's words, turning his head away for a few moments to regain his composure.

"You are not useless to her," he said when he turned back. "Far from it. That is why I am here. Elizabeth will need money. I told her I would speak with you and see what you can do."

"Ah, well, that I can arrange at least. A decent sum to travel with and a more permanent arrangement when she is settled. When is it to happen?"

"Tuesday."

"So soon!"

"It cannot be later. They are due to leave for Kinnell's estate on Thursday. She will be at the theatre for the royal performance and is going to try to slip away from him."

"Very well, I'll have trust papers drawn up straightaway. Ah, David lad"—he shook his head, his expression distraught—"I am her father. I should be able to protect her, but the only thing I am good for is making fine speeches in court. And what use is that? The law cannot mend some wrongs."

"The law cannot mend this," David agreed. "But *we* will mend it, I hope. Now, listen. There is one more thing I need to tell you."

"More than this?"

"Yes. I have a friend who will be helping me. His name is Euan MacLennan. He is a journalist, a Scot who lives in London. He has already met Elizabeth—he saw immediately that she was being mistreated and made it known to me he wished to help her. I will ensure that Elizabeth gets away from Kinnell on Tuesday evening, but it will be Euan, who will take her out of Scotland. He has friends in London who will help her settle into a new life."

"You know this man? Trust him?"

"Yes, with my life."

Chalmers took a deep breath. "What can I say, then? The man *I* entrusted her to is a monster." He paused. "Will you promise to check on her once she is settled, to ensure that she is well? I know I ask too much of you, lad, more than a man should ask of someone who is not his son, but there is no one I trust more."

"Of course. I will do everything I can to ensure she is safe."

"Thank you. Now, your Mr. MacLennan will have expenses to defray and Elizabeth will need coin before she can access any trust funds," Chalmers said. He unlocked his desk drawer and reached inside to draw out a metal box from which he lifted a handful of small, leather purses. He handed them to David. "There are ten guineas in each of those. Give them to Elizabeth and your friend."

"I will see they get them."

Chalmers put his hand over David's this time. "I will never be able to thank you enough if you get my girl away from that brute," he said softly.

"Just pray we are successful," David replied.

"I will do nothing but pray till I hear she is safe."

David felt a momentary panic after the interview with Chalmers—would Euan have changed his mind? Had he raised Chalmers's hopes unforgivably?

He needn't have worried. He opened his door that evening to find Euan on the other side, his expression anxious.

"Well?"

"She was there," David said. "Come in, and I'll tell you everything."

Euan's relief was so palpable he looked about ready to collapse from it. He followed David into the parlour, refusing his offer of whisky. "What did she say?"

David recited the details of his discussion with

Elizabeth. Then he told Euan about the conversation with Chalmers and passed him the purses of coin.

"I don't want these," Euan said, sounding almost offended. He made to toss them back, and David held up his hand.

"I won't allow you to help unless you agree to use those coins," David said, implacable.

"What? Why?" Euan bridled with offence.

"Firstly, because it is Chalmers's prerogative to help his own daughter and it is the only way he *can* help. And secondly, because the last thing Elizabeth needs at this moment is to feel beholden to another male—or more than she needs to, anyway."

Euan thought about that. "All right," he said at last, nodding. "I can see the sense in what you say, and I have no wish to make anything more difficult for her than it needs to be."

"Good. Let us discuss how we will arrange things, then. The streets around the theatre will be very congested, and it will be imperative that you get away quickly."

Euan had thought about it already. He'd planned a route by coach that went west then south, rather than taking the more direct east-coast route to London. With Chalmers's money he could do even better: hire a private carriage, at least for the first part of the journey, significantly reducing the risk of discovery at one of the main coaching inns.

"You could have a carriage wait for you near the theatre, not too near but perhaps on Regent Road," David said. "We only need to separate her from Kinnell for a few minutes to get her away. The crowds on the streets will swallow you both up quick enough, and ten minutes' walk will take you to Regent Road."

Euan nodded. "Where shall I meet you and when? The crowds will be as much a hindrance as a help, I expect. And there will be soldiers who will want to know why I'm loitering around a building that has the King in it."

"I had very little time to speak with Elizabeth at the ball—we had to make some sort of plan, so I said she should make her way to the front doors at half past nine. Aim to be near the front doors of the theatre a few minutes before that. Loitering round the back will be too suspicious and probably impossible to boot." He paused. "And Euan—"

"Yes?"

"Be watchful. Take care you are not followed."

Euan frowned. He stared at David for several long moments. "That's the second time you've mentioned the possibility of someone following me. Why?"

David stared back, his mind in turmoil. He had not wanted to break Murdo's confidence—and since Euan had been planning nothing untoward, it hadn't seemed so terrible to keep the full truth from him. But now things were different. Elizabeth's flight was at stake, and Euan *would* be acting suspiciously, lingering near the doors of a building the King would eventually emerge from.

He took a deep breath. "The truth is—the truth is I've been told you're on a list of troublemakers being watched by Crown agents. It's possible you are being followed, but I don't know for sure."

Euan's jaw tightened, and his angry gaze was an accusation. "You knew this? And you didn't tell me till now?"

"I'm sorry. I was told in confidence, and I thought that if you were only writing and not planning to break the law—"

"For God's sake, Davy, if someone's following me, it isn't to see if I break the law! It's to see who I meet with, who I talk to. It's to identify other 'troublemakers' and watch them too!"

David stared at Euan, dismayed. Murdo had said that too, hadn't he?

"If you're seen with MacLennan, it might affect you. Guilt by association…"

The fact was, when Euan had turned up at David's door, David could no more have turned him away than he could have turned away his own brother. He'd taken the risk of association willingly. But now it struck him forcibly that it wasn't only himself that may have been affected. Anyone else that Euan had met with may have fallen under suspicion.

"Christ!" he breathed, his voice shaking. "You're right. I should have told you."

Euan's angry expression softened. He sighed.

"Ah, Davy." He put a hand on David's arm. "You don't need to worry about anyone but yourself, all right? I've seen barely anyone since I came back to Scotland." He squeezed David's arm briefly, then let go. "And now you've told me, I'll be sure to shake them off. God knows I've had to do it before, and more than once."

David sent him a watery smile. "All right, but be careful. This might be Elizabeth's only chance."

Euan nodded. "I know that. I know it all too well."

Chapter Sixteen

Tuesday, 27th August, 1822

David had arranged to meet Murdo at seven o'clock on the night of the royal performance. They were meeting at the foot of North Bridge, a few minutes' walk from the Theatre Royal.

As he drew near to their meeting place, David began to grow concerned at the numbers of people thronging the streets. Even as far from the theatre as this, there were dense crowds milling, and whilst the general mood was elated, there was a distinct edge of aggression, doubtless fuelled by the ale and spirits that were flowing freely. Murdo was already waiting when David arrived, as splendid as always in his elegant garb, but with a frown on his handsome face.

"Apparently the theatre has been practically under siege since three o'clock this afternoon," he told David after greeting him. "They opened the doors to let some patrons in a few minutes ago, and there was nearly a riot."

"What? Why? Is someone protesting against the

King?"

"Not at all," Murdo replied. "From what I can make out, it's because it's the King's last public engagement and they all want in, but since there are seats inside for only one in twenty of this crowd, it's beginning to get rather ugly." A hesitant smile tugged the corner of his expressive mouth, and he raised one dark brow. "We don't *have* to go, I suppose. You could come straight to my house instead. We could have an early supper."

A bolt of panic ran through David at that suggestion. "I thought you had a box," he blurted out.

"I do," Murdo conceded. "But we've still got to fight our way through the crowd," He gestured at the sea of people stretching from where they stood to the doors of the Theatre Royal, and hopelessness surged in David. What if Elizabeth didn't come? What if Kinnell turned their carriage around and took her home?

"If you'd really rather not fight your way through the crowds, I don't mind going alone," David said. Too late he realised how ungrateful that sounded. Worse, how hurtful. As though he didn't even want Murdo's company.

Murdo stared at him in silence for a long, uncomfortable moment. When he finally spoke in a flat, calm voice, it was to say, "Of course I'll come. You are my guest."

"Murdo, I'm sorr—"

But Murdo just cut him off, striding past him. "Come on, then, if we don't get a move on, you're going to miss everything, and I wouldn't want you to feel deprived."

He began to push his way through the throng, earning himself some ripe curses in the process, and David followed in his wake, heartsore.

As they drew closer to the theatre—though still a good way off the main doors—it grew more difficult. The crowd was tightly packed here, none of them willing to give an inch.

Just then a man's voice behind them gave a loud bellow. "Make way!"

David turned his head and saw the voice came from a coachman. He was walking his horses right into the crowd, his whip held aloft in a blatantly threatening manner. Men and women scuttled out of his way, cursing him. Someone hurled a stone. It hit one of the horses on its flank, making the beast toss its head and pull against the traces. The coachman had to stand in his seat and haul at the reins to stop it rearing. David leapt back, pushing at Murdo's shoulder to get him out of the way of the panicky animal.

"Move aside!" the coachman shouted, swiping his whip at a man standing close by. David would have admired his reckless pluck if he hadn't found the man's attitude so offensive.

At that moment, a head popped out of the window of the carriage. At first all David saw was a handsome red-and-gold shako topped with an ostentatious black plume. Then his gaze moved down, and he saw that the owner of the shako wore a wicked smile, white teeth glinting under a splendid moustache.

It was Captain Sinclair.

"I say, Lord Murdo!" The captain grinned. "Whatever are you doing out here? This riffraff are waiting for the cheap seats. Don't you have a box? Oh, and it's your prodigy! Mr. Latimer, isn't it?"

"Fuckin' nerve!" someone beside David exclaimed. "Callin' me riffraff!"

Sinclair turned his grin on the offended man—a big man with hands like hammers. "No offence intended," he said with a twinkle that disappeared when the man made a noise like an angry bull. "Come on, Lord Murdo, in you get. You too, Latimer. Cunningham will have us at the doors in a jiffy." He opened the door of the carriage, and before David could protest, Murdo had dived inside, pulling David in behind him by the collar of his coat. They toppled down onto the floor of the carriage while Sinclair quickly closed the door and snicked the window shut.

Something slammed into the door an instant later, followed by another bellow of "Fuckin' nerve!" A few shouts of agreement chorused this conclusion, and then the coach was creaking forward again, punctuated by the coachman yelling at the crowd again.

David got to his feet and sat down, taking the empty bench opposite the captain, while Murdo settled into the space next to their host.

"Your coachman's going to harm someone out there," David snapped as he dusted his clothes off. "One of the horses was spooked by the crowd and looked ready to rear. We had to jump out of the way. It is beyond reckless to plough into them like this."

The captain just laughed, uncowed. "Don't fuss, Mr. Latimer. These are the calmest horses you could hope to find. I'd happily take them on a battlefield."

"It's Lauriston," Murdo said. "Not Latimer." His voice sounded oddly tight.

Sinclair sent Murdo an interested look. "Lauriston," he said as though weighing up the name, then turned to David and said lightly, "My apologies, Mr. Lauriston."

"No apology necessary," David replied, shrugging.

"*Do* you have a box?" Sinclair asked Murdo then.

"Yes."

"Might I join you?" Sinclair wheedled. "I was going to share Lord and Lady McInroy's, but McInroy's a terrible bore and I'd lief as not, if you could accommodate me."

Murdo hesitated for a barely perceptible instant. "Of course," he said eventually, and David felt a flush begin to rise up his neck. Brief as Murdo's pause had been, David had noticed it and heard the note of reluctance, and he rather thought, from the one-sided smile tickling the captain's mouth, that Sinclair had too.

"Excellent." He turned to David. "Do you know what the play is, Mr. Lauriston?"

"*Rob Roy*," David answered.

"Ah, one of Sir Walter's works. I should have guessed. The King loves them. Will the play be very different from the novel, do you suppose?"

"I wouldn't have thought so," David answered vaguely, though he really had no idea.

On the other side of the carriage, Murdo stared at them, his dark brows drawn together in a frown. He remained silent while Sinclair chattered to David, asking him whether he'd enjoyed the ball on Saturday and how he'd liked the dancing, the music, the supper.

David could see how a man like this could become a King's favourite at so young an age. He was a pleasure to talk to, with his sparkling eyes, ready smile and amusing conversation. He could see too that there was more to him than this happy and pleasing exterior. The blue eyes that twinkled so easily held a keen intelligence and a watchfulness that was belied by his careless manner.

It was another few minutes before the coachman thumped on the roof of the carriage to signify they had reached the doors of the theatre.

"Ready to charge when I give the order?" Sinclair asked with a grin.

"This is not one of your battlefields, Sinclair," Murdo said dryly.

"Don't you believe it," the captain replied, half rising from his seat. "This mob might adore the King right now, but it could turn on us all in the blink of an eye. We're as close to revolution now as we've ever been, gentlemen. Can't you just taste it in the air?" His eyes sparkled, as though the prospect of revolution was positively delightful.

He stood up, then, rocking the carriage in the process, and threw the door open, jumping down and almost knocking over an old man in a drab coat that had seen better days. The man's shabby appearance was brightened by a smart, new-looking saltire cockade on his lapel. He let out a yell when Sinclair all but fell on top of him.

"I beg your pardon, sir," the captain said apologetically, brushing the man's coat down with a brisk arm movement. His actions managed to elicit an answering smile from the old man, even as Sinclair manoeuvred him deftly out of the way and moved forward to knock at the closed doors of the theatre, Murdo and David a step behind.

A moment later, a slot in the door shot open, revealing a suspicious male face. On seeing the captain's splendid uniform and Murdo's elegance, the suspicion faded away to be replaced by an expression of obsequious pleasure that only deepened when Murdo stated his name and informed the man that he had a box waiting for him.

"Please stand aside while I open the door, my lord," the doorkeeper said. "We are not allowing any of this mob in till His Majesty has arrived and is seated, but those that have a *box* may make themselves comfortable and call for refreshments in the meantime." He opened the door by the merest crack, obliging them to squeeze themselves through the tiny gap, then closed and bolted the door behind them.

The doorkeeper transpired to be an elderly man in moth-eaten highland apparel that looked more like an old theatre costume than anything else. All the colour had faded out of the fabric, turning what would once have been a red-and-green plaid to something that looked more like pink and blue. The sporran that hung at the front of the man's kilt looked even worse—like one of the dead rats David's father's terrier used to bring out of the barn at home, clamped between its jaws.

The doorkeeper clicked his fingers, and a boy—similarly bedecked in faded tartan—appeared to lead the way up the winding stairs to Murdo's box. After three long flights of wooden steps, they reached the floor that led to the boxes. Halfway along the corridor, the boy stopped, opening the heavy velvet curtains with a distinctly theatrical flourish and ushering them inside. Murdo flipped a coin to the boy as they walked past him. He caught it and pocketed it with a grin, gave a brief bobbing bow and left them, promising someone would come to take their refreshments order directly.

Inside, the box was positively luxurious, and David guessed it must be one of the best in the theatre. The floor was carpeted with a heavy Turkish rug and furnished with four gilt-painted chairs and a small table to hold their refreshments. The curtains at the back kept any draught off.

David stepped forward to the edge of the box, curling his fingers over gilded and moulded plasterwork as he scrutinised the other boxes, some of which were already occupied. Was Elizabeth here yet? he wondered. Would she come at all?

He could see no sign either of her or of Kinnell. Not yet.

"Mr. Lauriston, would you care to sit by me?"

David turned his head. Sinclair had made himself comfortable on one of the chairs, his long legs stretched out and his black boots gleaming. He'd discarded his shako on the chair to his right, and his hands cradled the back of his dark head, scarlet-clad elbows sticking out.

He really was a very comely man.

The captain raised a questioning brow and gestured

to the empty chair to his left with a jerk of his head.

David wondered where Sinclair wanted Murdo to sit. Presumably on the fourth chair, on the other side of his ridiculous hat.

Whatever the captain's views were, Murdo had other ideas. He lifted the shako up by its black plume and tossed it at Sinclair, sitting himself down in its place.

"This is *my* box, and Mr. Lauriston is *my* guest," he said. "He will sit beside me."

For a moment, David just stared at him, astonished by his blatant possessiveness.

"Ah, so it's like that, is it?" Sinclair said archly.

David opened his mouth to demur, but before he could get a word out, Murdo replied, "Yes. It is." He gave the captain a steady look, a distinct challenge in his gaze.

Sinclair chuckled. "I did rather wonder," he admitted. "And I don't blame you for warning me off, Murdo. He's awfully fetching, this one."

A hot flash of colour invaded David's cheeks as he absorbed the captain's words and his gaze snapped to Murdo, his heart beginning to race.

Murdo held up a hand. "Don't worry," he said quietly. "Captain Sinclair shares our preferences. And he's not as reckless as he appears—I've known him a long time. You can trust him."

You can trust him.

That reassurance from Murdo—Murdo who had no idea as to David's real purpose here tonight—made David's throat tighten and guilt bloom in his gut. He wished, suddenly, he could confess it all. Perhaps he would have done, if the captain wasn't sitting there, regarding the two of them with interested amusement.

Instead, David nodded once, then crossed the box and took the chair next to Murdo. After a moment, he let his knee loll against Murdo's, welcoming the tiny contact, wishing he could have more.

He glanced at Murdo. The other man stared straight ahead, but one of those rare, genuine smiles of his was just tickling the corner of his mouth. He must have felt David's gaze upon him, because he turned his head and their gazes met, and Murdo's smile—still small and somewhat secret—deepened. Deepened, oddly, without widening. Deepened in his dark eyes; in the gaze that gentled as it moved over David's face.

On the other side of Murdo, the captain sighed heavily.

"I should've stayed with the McInroys," he muttered.

Over the next hour, the finest seats in the Theatre Royal slowly filled with Edinburgh's best and brightest. Sinclair secured them two bottles of something that professed to be champagne but tasted rather like David's mother's cider.

"You're quiet tonight," Murdo murmured in David's ear at one point.

"Am I?" David replied, feeling guilty. He was so absorbed in watching for Elizabeth he could barely concentrate on the conversation in the box. He checked his watch for the umpteenth time. Soon enough he'd be making his excuses, slipping away to try to find her, wherever she may be.

It hadn't really occurred to him till now that he'd be leaving Murdo to his own devices when he did that. But then, perhaps it wouldn't take so very long? Perhaps he and Elizabeth would slip out easily, find Euan, and he'd return to his seat beside Murdo with no one the wiser.

Or perhaps not.

David ran through a hundred scenarios in his mind as he watched and waited, and all the while he was bothered by that nagging sense of guilt that had first struck him when Murdo suggested they miss the performance altogether and that had been growing in him ever since.

Perhaps he should tell Murdo about the business with Elizabeth. Just do it now. He'd understand; he'd already tried to help Elizabeth once before.

But no, it would be unfair to draw him into this, and foolish, with Sinclair sitting there. And it should be a simple matter, really. The fewer people who knew, the better.

A sudden warmth on the back of his hand made

him startle. It was Murdo's hand, resting briefly on his own, squeezing gently.

"Are you all right?" Murdo whispered in his ear. "You look worried."

David nodded. "I'm fine," he lied.

As Murdo went to withdraw his hand, David turned his own over so their hands were palm to palm. He tangled his fingers with Murdo's in a brief caress, and Murdo lingered too, neither of them willing to break the contact even as their hands drew apart and Murdo returned his hand to his own knee.

It was only a few minutes later that David caught a flutter of movement in the box opposite their own, a box that had sat empty all evening till now. Its occupants had finally arrived, and when David turned his head, he saw them.

Elizabeth. And Kinnell.

Kinnell was seating Elizabeth, his every movement a study in uxoriousness as he rearranged her shawl around her shoulders and murmured in her ear. Elizabeth's expression was blank, closed. Her eyes drifted, drifted...

And then she was looking at David, her shoulders going rigid, her eyes wide and pleading, unseen by her husband.

She mouthed three words, slowly, deliberately. Unmissable.

Half. Past. Nine.

When the King arrived, the orchestra began to play a medley of Scottish airs to welcome him. Once he was safe in his box, surrounded by his inner circle, the theatre management let the wider public in to file into the cheaper seats.

The ordinary people of the town thronged inside, chattering loudly and singing, bringing the place to messy life.

When everyone that was going to get in was inside and the doors were closed once again, there was a great cheer. The King waved from his box in that benign way of his, and in response, the crowd cheered again and waved back with whatever they had, handkerchiefs and scarves, hats and ribbons.

This went on for a few minutes, till the curtains opened to reveal the cast of the play, already in costume. The orchestra struck up the national anthem, and everyone began to sing, an emotional swelling of song, complete with a new verse composed especially for the King's visit. Unfortunately, no one seemed to know the words to the extra verse.

Then, and only then, did the performance begin.

David barely noticed what was happening on stage. He checked his watch practically every five minutes. *Half past nine.* Only now did it occur to David how very thin their plan was. Thin and ill thought out. Doomed. How would they find Euan in that vast crowd? How would Elizabeth ever get away from

Kinnell? The man was still standing behind her—*standing* when there were three chairs he could have taken his pick of. One of his gloved hands rested on her shoulder, a constant reminder; a chain made flesh.

David was aware of Murdo and the captain talking occasionally, sotto voce. From time to time, Murdo murmured something in David's ear too, and David would give a distracted smile or nod in return. He realised he was entirely failing to act normally but was powerless to do better.

At twenty-five minutes past nine, David glanced at the box opposite and saw Elizabeth rising from her seat. She walked two paces before Kinnell's hand shot out to grasp her wrist. Turning her head, she whispered something in his ear and made to walk away again, but he kept his grip on her wrist, and a visible tension stiffened the arm that held her in place. For a moment, he held her firm, but although they were alone in the box, they were visible to everyone in the theatre and Kinnell knew it. When she tugged again, he let her go, watching her as she disappeared through the curtains at the back of their box.

David stood then, and Murdo frowned up at him, surprised. He leaned over and said in Murdo's ear, "I feel a little warm. I'm going to get some air."

Murdo looked unconvinced, but David forced himself to move away without further explanation, stepping quickly towards the curtains and slipping through the gap in the middle.

Once outside the box, he moved quickly, hurrying down the first two flights of stairs to the common gallery, where he found Elizabeth. She was hovering anxiously. Her worried expression eased a little when she saw him, and she stepped towards him.

"Thank God!" she exclaimed as they came together. "I don't have long. He may follow me—I made him angry."

"Come on, then." David grabbed her hand, and they tripped down the last flight of steps together. They were almost at the bottom when a commanding voice, far above them, called out, "Elizabeth! Where are you?"

Elizabeth froze and looked up at David in fear.

"Ignore him," David said. "He's further up, and we'll be out of here in a moment."

For a couple of vital seconds, Elizabeth stood, locked in fear, while Kinnell's boot heels clicked on the wooden steps above them, bringing him closer.

"Come on!" David whispered, tugging her hand. "If you don't go now, I may never be able to help you again."

Her expression shifted then from fear to determination, and she nodded. They took the last few stairs quickly and tumbled into the foyer at the bottom, where they found the same doorkeeper as before, pacing the floor in front of the closed door that kept the crowd outside at bay.

"Open the door," David demanded, striding towards him, Elizabeth's hand still in his own.

"I can't do that!" the doorkeeper replied. "Have you seen the crowd out there? We could only let a tenth in and the rest aren't happy—I'm not opening that door till the play's finished."

"Open it now!" David snapped, and he must've sounded serious because the little man jumped and began to get his keys out.

"Stop there!"

At the sound of that dictatorial voice, David threw a glance over his shoulder. Kinnell was just coming round the bend of the last flight of stairs. He only had another dozen steps to go and the foyer to cross and he'd be on their heels.

"No, no!" Elizabeth moaned.

The doorkeeper had just inserted the key in the lock. David pushed him aside, took hold of the key and thrust it home, grinding it in the lock. It was stiff, but he wrenched at it until the lock gave, and then he was shoving the door open, pushing Elizabeth out in front of him and slamming it behind them.

The crowd David had been expecting to dive into wasn't there. The steps that led to the street from the theatre doors were clear, and at the bottom of them stood a line of fine carriages waiting for His Majesty's emergence from the theatre. The crowd had been pushed well back from the carriages and was being kept in place by a line of the King's personal guard of troops. Euan had to be in there somewhere—somewhere in that throng.

"Come on," David said, lunging forward, pulling Elizabeth behind him. But before they'd gone a few steps, the door behind them opened with a crash.

"Elizabeth!"

David met Elizabeth's terrified gaze. "You have to run," he told her, pushing her towards the steps. "I'll hold him back while you find Euan. Go."

This time she didn't hesitate, just lifted her skirts and ran down the steps to the street below while David turned to face Kinnell, who was right behind him, his face twisted and red with anger.

"You again!" he yelled in harsh disbelief. "Get out of my way!"

David pitched himself at Kinnell, wrapping his arms around the other man, determined to stop him getting to Elizabeth.

Kinnell's fist connected with his stomach, and he grunted, air rushing out of him. His feet stumbled, slipping on the stairs, and they fell together, tumbling to the bottom of the steps where the carriages stood.

The fall knocked the wind out of David, but he still hung on to the other man. *Run*, he thought. *Run.*

"Let go of me, you bastard! She is my *wife*!" Kinnell shouted, landing another punch.

The pain of that blow to David's kidneys was astonishing, but even though his arms felt like porridge now, he kept his arms clamped round Kinnell's body.

"David!"

A new voice this time. Murdo.

David twisted his head, looking up the steps to where Murdo stood at the theatre doors, eyes wide as he took in the sight of David brawling in the street.

Kinnell took advantage of David's momentary inattention, breaking out of David's arms and stuttering to his feet.

"Elizabeth!" he yelled as he surged forward, and David somehow knew from the tone of his voice that Kinnell could see her, that he had his sights set on her now.

By some miracle, David managed to lurch to his feet again, lungs labouring, shoes scrabbling against the slippery cobbles, body protesting. He lunged after Kinnell, a headlong leap of desperation, and grabbed at the tail of Kinnell's coat, grasping just enough of a handhold to slow the other man down again.

Kinnell swung round in David's grip, his expression murderous now. His hands came up, and he thrust David violently away from him. The shove sent David staggering backwards. Back, back, into empty air, his arms cartwheeling for a moment.

For that moment—or maybe forever—David was suspended there, in the act of falling. Falling, to the sound of panicked whinnying and someone shouting. Falling, under the immense shadow of a carriage horse as it reared in its traces.

The falling ended with a slamming pain.

Then nothing.

Chapter Seventeen

Waking—when he woke—was to enter a world of pain, and so much of it he couldn't pinpoint where it began or ended.

He tried to resist consciousness, until a familiar voice said, "He's stirring." A familiar voice that thrummed with fear.

He couldn't settle on a name for the voice, but it summoned an image of strong fingers entwined with his own. A secret, irrepressible smile. By an immense effort, he managed to crack an eyelid open.

A man was bending over him, his dark hair dishevelled, his eyes red-rimmed and bloodshot.

"David, thank God! Can you speak?"

He shifted, and the pain was agonising. A whimper was all he could manage. He sounded like an animal.

"Don't move—" the man said at once, then looked over his shoulder. "Is that draught ready yet?"

When he turned back, he said, "I thought you were dead—" and his voice cracked on the last word.

Murdo.

David tried to say the name, to show Murdo that he knew him, but all he managed was another broken whimper.

A second man arrived beside Murdo. He was much older, with sparse grey hair that failed to cover his shiny scalp.

"Support his head, my lord," this man said, his voice quietly commanding. "He will find it difficult to drink this and it will spill, but we only need get some into him, then he will sleep, and we will see what to do."

Murdo slid a hand under David's shoulders and lifted him, just a little, but it was enough that every nerve in David's body screamed. Every nerve, but not his mouth. Again, the only noise that came from him was tiny animal sounds.

"I'm sorry," Murdo whispered. "God, I'm sorry, David."

The older man used one hand to press on David's chin, opening his jaw, and the other to tip the rim of a bowl against his bottom lip. Bitter liquid flooded his mouth, too much to swallow. It flowed out of his mouth and down the sides of his face, but some of it hit the back of his throat, and he gagged on it, swallowing and choking weakly. Again it flowed. Again.

"Enough," the man said at last.

The strong arm under his shoulders was gently withdrawn, and he was lowered to a flat position again. The impossible, unbearably intense pain that had flared when he was lifted subsided into something lesser, something that gradually began to feel more and more bearable as he continued to lie there and the draught did its work.

The edges of his vision greyed. Oblivion called him back to his rest.

The next time he opened his eyes, he knew where he was. The curving plasterwork petals of the ceiling rose told him this was Murdo's bedchamber.

"David, you're awake."

He turned towards the voice, wincing at the slamming pain in his head that accompanied the sudden movement.

Murdo sat beside him. He looked utterly wrecked, grey circles under his bloodshot eyes, his hair standing up on end where he'd run his hands through it.

"Murdo—" David's voice came out dry and cracked, and he wondered suddenly how the rest of him was faring. He moved as though to begin sitting up, to check himself. Murdo immediately leaned forward, placing one large, warm hand on his chest.

"Easy, there."

It was then that another thought—another person—occurred to him.

"Elizabeth?" he breathed.

"Gone," Murdo replied. "Kinnell was seized by the King's soldiers after you were felled by that horse. She ran away and hasn't been seen since."

"Thank God," David whispered. It hadn't been for nothing, at least.

"I don't know why you're thanking God," Murdo replied, his jaw set and grim. "You managed to nearly kill yourself, you idiot."

"How bad?" David croaked. He strained his neck off the pillow to look down at himself, only to fall back from the sudden intense pain in his head.

"*Jesus Christ!*" he hissed.

"Careful! Your head was clipped by the horse's hoof, and there's a fracture—though you're lucky your skull wasn't entirely caved in."

"No wonder it hurts," David mumbled.

"That's not all, I'm afraid," Murdo said. "Your right leg was broken in two places. Luckily, you were out cold when it was being set."

David felt a surge of fear. A bad break could be difficult to heal. He might even lose his leg. He lifted his head again, panic keeping him going through the pain this time, pain that eased when Murdo jumped up and braced his arm behind David to support his head and neck.

David looked down his body, at the unexpected bulk under the bedcovers.

"Show me," he demanded desperately, his voice

near breaking.

Murdo leaned forward, using his free hand to pull the covers back. "It's not so bad," he murmured. "Just splinted and bandaged. You need to rest and let it heal."

David barely heard him. He was too busy staring at his leg. Not that you could tell that it *was* a leg. The whole length of it was bandaged and trussed up in what looked like a stiff wood-and-leather harness. He was immobilised. Unable to bend knee or ankle, the whole limb firmly held in position for healing.

"How long will it need to be like this?"

"At least three months, perhaps longer."

David gasped. "Three *months*—"

"It could be six. The physician says the bones need to knit properly before you can risk placing weight on it."

"I can't *manage* like this for six months—or even three!"

"I'm afraid you'll have to," Murdo replied. "It's a bad break, and if you're not careful, you'll get an infection in it—and then you'll be looking at amputation."

David made an incoherent noise, part protest, part despair, and turned his head into Murdo's shoulder, gulping in Murdo's familiar scent for a long, weak moment as he absorbed the reality of his situation.

Murdo shifted his body so that they sat side by

side, though with Murdo's strong arm still supporting David's back. He stroked the apple of David's shoulder with his thumb, murmuring, "Come on. It'll be all right."

"No, it won't. I really *can't* manage," David said, the words pouring out of him unchecked. "I can't get to court like this, or to the library. Christ, how will I even get *home*? My rooms are up two flights of stairs!" Every new thought was worse as he contemplated just how profound his new helplessness was. "I'll have to go back to Midlauder," he realised aloud. He pulled away from Murdo's shoulder and looked up at him, horrified. "I can't ask my mother to nurse me! She's got too many other things to do to be running after me again. And what about my clients, the practice I've built up—"

"David, please. You're panicking needlessly." Murdo's voice was calm and firm, and it halted David in his tracks. "I've already thought about all of this," he continued. "I want you to come with me, to my estate in Perth, to recuperate."

For a moment, David could only stare at him. "But my work—"

"Will be taken care of by Mr. Ferguson."

David paused. "Donald?" he said at last.

"The same. He came here yesterday. He was asking for you—and for news of his sister-in-law. We spoke for a while, and he said he'd do whatever was necessary to deal with your work while you get well again."

"He came yesterday? What day was that?" David frowned. "How long have I been unconscious?"

"Several days. I brought you here straight after the accident. You slept through Tuesday night and all of Wednesday. Today's Thursday and"—Murdo craned his neck to look at a clock on the mantelpiece—"it's almost noon now. And in all that time, you've only had a little water, so you must be starving. I'd better ring for some food." Murdo shifted, carefully beginning to extricate himself.

"Wait a moment," David said, and Murdo stilled behind him.

"What is it? Are you in pain?"

He breathed out a shaky laugh. "Well, yes, but that's not it. I just need to... Murdo, I'm so—" He broke off, incoherent, embarrassed when tears sprang to his eyes. "Just—thank you."

"What for?"

"For everything," David said. "Taking care of me, bringing me here. You didn't need to do that."

Murdo went very silent. At last he said, "You don't need to thank me."

"I do. I can't even imagine what would've happened to me if you hadn't been there. Where I would have ended up. Maybe even dead."

Murdo shook his head at that, a fierce repudiation of David's grim prediction. "I just wish"—he paused—

"I just wish that you'd told me what you were planning beforehand. Didn't you think I'd help you?"

David sighed. "I didn't want to involve you."

"You involved Euan MacLennan," Murdo replied flatly.

David stilled. "How do you know that?"

"Donald Ferguson said he was part of the plan. What was he doing? Waiting for her outside?"

David nodded.

Murdo went silent, but there was a tension in him that David could feel. After a minute, Murdo blurted out, "I can't believe you trusted him more than me. After what he did to you."

"What do you mean, 'what he did to me'?"

"What do you think I mean? I'm talking about two years ago. About him holding a gun to your head and threatening to kill you. Don't you remember that night?" His voice held disbelieving scorn.

"I remember," David said quietly. "But I always understood why Euan did that. He is—he is a good man, Murdo."

"I hope you're right, because you've entrusted a vulnerable young woman to his care."

"I do trust him. And besides that, he's in love with her. He'd protect her with his last breath."

"Love!" Murdo huffed out the word on a scornful laugh. David wasn't sure what to make of that.

"I trust him," David repeated.

There was a long pause, a pregnant silence.

"Do you trust *me*?" Murdo asked. He sounded almost diffident, as though the answer to his question was of little more than passing interest.

But when David whispered, "There's no one I trust more, I think," the tension in him seemed to drain away.

"You need to eat," Murdo said after a few minutes. "I'll get some broth brought up for you."

He began to shift till David put a hand on his leg, staying him. "Don't go yet."

Murdo didn't say anything in reply, but he stayed where he was, and they sat there for a while after, Murdo's long fingers still stroking David's shoulder.

Chalmers came the next afternoon.

David had been moved to a long couch in the study. He was reading a volume of essays when Murdo looked in.

"Mr. Chalmers is here," Murdo said. "Donald Ferguson's with him, but Chalmers wants to talk to you alone first. Do you feel up to it?"

"Yes, of course," David said, bracing himself on his elbow and pulling himself painfully into a more upright position. As well as a fractured skull and broken leg, he had bruised his ribs, and they screamed with agony whenever he moved.

Murdo nodded and withdrew. A few minutes later, he returned with Chalmers on his arm. The older man's gait was slow and painful. He seemed worse—markedly so—from when David had last seen him.

"You shouldn't be out," David scolded, and Chalmers grimaced.

"I had to see you," the older man said. "Before you go to Perthshire."

Murdo helped Chalmers settle into the armchair next to David's couch. "I'll leave you alone to talk," he said diplomatically and withdrew.

Chalmers stared at the closed door for a moment after Murdo left. "He's been very kind to you," he said.

David couldn't read anything in the older man's tone. In the end, he simply agreed, offering no explanation. "Yes, he has."

"A good friend," Chalmers concluded. "If an unexpected one."

"Very true," David agreed and smiled, more to himself than at Chalmers.

"I'm so sorry this happened to you," Chalmers said without further preamble. "All because you were helping my girl."

"I'm just glad she got away."

"I've had a note from her," Chalmers said. "It arrived yesterday morning." He fished in his pocket and drew it out, handing it to David.

The quality of the paper was poor and the writing slapdash.

Dearest Papa,

You will know by now that I have run away from K.

Thank you for the money you sent for me by way of D L. It means more to me than mere gold—to know you love me still is the greatest blessing I could ask for.

Know that I am safe and well. I am travelling with a kind man who is a friend of D L's. He will see me safely settled when we arrive at our destination. As soon as I can, I will write to you properly and send you my direction.

Send me news of D L when you write. I pray all is well with him, and that K has not harmed him in retribution for helping me.

I love you, Papa. My greatest wish is to see you again, one day.

Your loving daughter,
E

When David looked up, Chalmers had tears in his eyes.

"She doesn't know what happened to you," Chalmers said. "She'd probably have refused to leave town if she'd known. She was always...very fond of you, lad." His voice carried regret. Sorrow. "For a while, I thought the two of you might marry. It would have made me so happy if you had. Instead, Elizabeth is run to London, and you are injured." He sounded pained when he added, "All because of her impetuous decision to marry that brute, Kinnell."

"Don't blame Elizabeth for that," David said. "If anyone is to blame, it is I. In truth, she had hopes of me, and I did not come up to scratch. I disappointed her. Had I not done so, she would never have married him."

There, he'd said it at last: admitted his guilt at failing Elizabeth. He looked at Chalmers expecting to see anger, but all he saw was regret and pity.

"Ah, I see. Well, we are none of us perfect, are we?"

"Far from it. But at least Elizabeth is away from him now. And she is strong, Chalmers. She will find a way to make a new life for herself. One in which she can be happy again."

"Do you think so? I worry. A woman who has run from her husband is beyond society, and Elizabeth is all alone now."

David shook his head. "She is not alone. She is with Euan MacLennan. He will not abandon her. He is not going back to some conventional life that an unexplained woman cannot fit into. He is…" David paused, thinking how to say this. "Well, he is what they call a free thinker. He will continue to help Elizabeth when they reach London, you can be sure of that."

"A free thinker?" Chalmers sounded dubious.

David smiled, understanding the older man's reservations. "Yes. For example, he believes that women and men are equal. That a man should not be able to command his wife in marriage, only love her."

Chalmers frowned. "He sounds like more than a free thinker. He sounds like a radical."

"He's that too," David admitted, driven to honesty. "He believes in universal suffrage and educating the masses and taking children out of factories—all those unthinkable heresies." He smiled to show his sympathy with Euan's ideals. "And that's why he's *exactly* the sort of man you should want to travel with Elizabeth—someone who respects her as a person in her own right and will not take advantage of a woman on her own."

Chalmers was quiet for a while. Then he said, "So long as he does right by Elizabeth, I'll be eternally grateful to him."

"He will," David assured him. "He is an honourable man, and he did not undertake this task lightly."

"Do you think he will be able to protect her if Kinnell finds her?"

"I hope it will not come to that," David said. "But if it does, I have no doubt Euan will do his utmost."

"There is certainly a chance it will come to that," Chalmers said heavily. "Kinnell is a possessive man. He has already been at my door to interrogate me. And not only about Elizabeth. He has discovered your identity. He knows that you and I have worked together over the last few years."

David frowned. "Do you think he realises you were complicit in Elizabeth's flight?"

"I am *sure* he does," Chalmers said stoutly. "I said very little, but he knows I do not like him and that I do not commiserate with him over her running away."

David smiled at that. He could well imagine Chalmers being uncommunicative, evasive and downright hostile. "I see no reason to worry too much," he said in a calm, certain tone. "Kinnell may search for her, but there is no reason to believe he will find her. Don't forget he has no idea where Elizabeth has gone, or who she is with. She might have gone north, south, east or west for all he knows. And Euan knows some things about hiding."

Chalmers sighed. "I hope so."

"The most important thing you can do for her now is to secure her financial independence. Have you made the arrangements for her we spoke about?"

Chalmers nodded. "I've a capital sum that's going in trust for her. My brother-in-law is a solicitor in London. He'll manage the trust and arrange regular payments to Elizabeth once I have her direction. All I need to do now is appoint the trustees so the trust deed can be finalised. It's imperative it's done as quickly as possible as I'm…not well." He paused, then added, "Donald has agreed to be one trustee. Will you be the other?"

David didn't hesitate. "Of course."

"Thank you. I'll have the papers finalised this afternoon, and then it will be done." He closed his eyes then, as though against pain or maybe exhaustion. When he opened them again, he said, "I'm so grateful to you, David. For everything. I'll never be able to tell you how much—"

"Please don't," David pleaded. He knew somehow that he would always be troubled by the nagging guilt that he might have spared Elizabeth all this if only he'd dealt with her feelings more gently.

Chalmers nodded and cleared his throat. Became businesslike. "Now, you mustn't worry about your practice," he said. "Donald is going to take care of everything while you heal. Are your case papers in your rooms? What's going on?"

David began to outline the work he had on hand. After a while, the door opened and Murdo stood there, Donald Ferguson at his shoulder.

"That's the twenty minutes that you asked for over," Murdo said, addressing Chalmers. "Are you ready for Mr. Ferguson to join you now?"

"Yes, yes, I'm sorry to have kept you both waiting. Donald, come in." Chalmers paused. "You may wish to join us too, my lord, if you have time to spare. We were just discussing how we manage Mr. Lauriston's life for the next few months while he gets better."

Murdo looked at David, a question in his dark gaze.

"I know you're dying to send a servant up to my rooms to pack my things," David said in a long-suffering tone. "So you may as well join us."

Murdo smiled. It was one of his rare smiles, and it made David's heart kick like a mule in his chest.

"You're right, of course, Lauriston," he said. "As usual, you're absolutely right."

Chapter Eighteen

Thursday, 5th September, 1822

The carriage journey to Perthshire was gruelling. Though not terribly far from Edinburgh, the roads were poor, and at the slow pace Murdo insisted upon, it took them the whole day to get there.

Murdo had hired a special carriage to take David. It was spacious inside with a specially made bench that David could recline upon, allowing his leg to stay completely still in its bindings. Murdo's servants had lined the bench with blankets and stocked it with pillows to make it as comfortable as possible for David.

Despite these efforts, the journey was still torturous. The roads were badly rutted and very narrow and winding. Even at a slow place, David felt like he was being constantly jolted and jarred. He couldn't even distract himself with reading since the constant movement nauseated him.

Murdo rode on horseback most of the way, but, on their last stop, he didn't take a new horse, choosing to join David in the carriage instead.

"Just ten more miles," he promised as he climbed in, "and the scenery on this last stretch is beautiful."

"How would I know? It's not as if I can see out the window," David griped. He hated the petulant tone of his own voice but he was tired and in pain and feeling sorry for himself, not just because of the discomfort of this journey, but at the thought of what lay ahead of him. He'd already had a week of enforced idleness, and it was driving him mad. He couldn't see how he'd bear three more months of this.

"You can see out the window if you sit up," Murdo said gently. "Let me help you."

He helped David into a sitting position that enabled his leg to remain stretched out and began to pile the pillows and blankets up behind him to provide support. But there just wasn't enough bulk to make good the gap between bench and wall. The reclining bench had been designed for someone to lie on, not sit up.

"I've already tried that," David said glumly as Murdo tried yet another combination.

Oddly, Murdo's mouth quirked up at his grumbling. "I've never seen you peevish before," he said, sounding amused.

A pang of guilt struck David. Murdo had done his utmost to make this journey as pleasant as possible. And all David could do was complain.

"I'm sorry," he sighed.

"Don't be. It's actually quite reassuring to see you being as human as the rest of us for once. You usually make me so aware of my own feet of clay."

David frowned. "You make me sound like a prig," he said. "Am I that bad?"

"No, just annoyingly virtuous at times," Murdo replied cheerfully. "Like when you tell me that life's about being true to yourself and I know you're being completely sincere."

Before David could respond to that, Murdo spoke again. "Oh, look, I've got it! If I sit up behind you, you can rest your back against my chest and you'll be able to see perfectly."

He threw the pillows he'd piled up out of the way and slid in behind David, wedging his big body into the space between the head of the bench and the back wall of the carriage. Then he wrapped his arms round David's chest, carefully pulling David back a little, till David's tailbone met his groin. David suppressed a moan, turning his attention instead to the carriage window through which he could indeed now see.

"Is that better?"

"Much, thank you. But what about you, aren't you terribly uncomfortable?"

"It's only ten miles, and"—Murdo dropped his lips to David's ear—"this position has its compensations."

David flushed, unsure how to respond. There had been nothing of that nature between them since his accident. How could there be with David so disabled? But the memory of the night that Murdo had fucked him haunted him constantly. And Murdo's proximity and kindness were fostering a new and different intimacy between them that hadn't existed before. There was friendship between them now, as well as the other. A regard that went beyond David's desire to hold a well-made male body against his own.

These new feelings were galling at times—like when he realised that he didn't want to share Murdo's attention with anyone else, and that it perturbed him that Murdo's head footman was so handsome... Or perhaps these absurd observations were nothing more than a mark of his forced indolence, of having too much time on his hands?

The carriage jerked forward, jolting them both and saving David from having to respond to Murdo's teasing remark, but there were still Murdo's arms around his chest and the warm huff of Murdo's breath at his ear to contend with. There was still the impossible-to-shake feeling of well-being and security that flooded him whenever Murdo was physically close to him.

It had been such a long, long time since he'd had anyone to lean on.

"We're about to turn down the hill that takes us into the glen," Murdo murmured in his ear. "That's when it begins to get more picturesque."

It was quite a steep hill, and David was glad to have Murdo holding him steady as the horses picked their way down. It would not have been a comfortable descent on his own, sliding around on the bench, trying to stay still.

At last they were at the bottom, and Murdo said, "Just look at that."

The glen stretched out before them, long and narrow and yellow-green, between two ranges of mountains. A river gushed through it, bubbling white and frothy over big black stones. Out of the corner of his eye David caught a flutter of movement and, turning his head, spied two peewits tumbling and wheeling in the sky.

He hadn't seen a peewit in years.

"What do you think?" Murdo said in his ear.

"It's beautiful," David answered honestly, even as his gaze tracked up the mountains and he thought with a pang, *I won't be able to go up there.*

Not for a while anyway.

"As soon as I saw it, I knew it was what I'd been looking for."

"Is this part of your estate, then?"

"Not quite. The border of my land begins about three miles from here. This is McNally's land. He's not very well disposed to me at the moment, but I hope to change that."

"Well, you can be very persuasive."

"Do you think so?" A soft laugh stirred the strands of hair at David's temple, sending a pleasurable shiver down his neck. The shiver made his whole back brush lightly against Murdo's chest, and the strong arms around David briefly tightened in response. Just that simple physical exchange made David feel suddenly happy and hopeful as he hadn't felt in years. Hopeful despite his crumbling career, and his money worries, and his physical injuries.

"Yes, and I should know," he teased. "None better. God knows I've been subjected to your persuasiveness often enough."

Another good-natured chuckle, then lips at his temple in a brief kiss.

A sigh.

"David."

Just his name. Not a question but a statement. Or maybe an answer.

David waited, allowing himself the silence and the arms about him as he did so.

"I thought you were dead," Murdo said at last.

David waited, but Murdo said no more, and at last he broke the silence himself. "I'm sorry if I caused you distress."

"Distress." Murdo laughed harshly, as though the word was absurd.

After a moment, he said, "I saw Kinnell push you, and you fell back. I just knew the horse was going to rear. I ran down the steps, but I couldn't get to you in time. I saw its hoof clip you, and you just dropped like a stone, and then the horse was stumbling all over you. I thought, *he's dead, he's dead*. I ran up to you, and you were so white, as though all the blood had just drained right out of you."

David didn't know what to say. He sifted through the threads of too many feelings, regret, anguish, but something too that felt oddly like happiness, to know that Murdo cared.

"The thought of you being dead—I realised I couldn't bear it. Bad enough not to have you. But for you not to be alive somewhere? That was—it was unthinkable."

David turned his head, suddenly needing to see Murdo, and for once, he didn't bother to mask his own feelings. Hell, he didn't know what his own feelings *were*, but he thought they might not be dissimilar to Murdo's, because he looked as overwhelmed and emotional as David felt.

"I don't know what this thing between us is," Murdo said, and he sounded genuinely bewildered. "But I can't give it up. I can't give *you* up."

"Murdo—"

David didn't know what else to say, so instead he raised one arm, curving it about Murdo's neck, and drew him down till their lips met. He kissed Murdo, and it was like water. Like something necessary and life-giving. Murdo's lips parted, and David deepened the kiss, for once the aggressor.

When Murdo finally raised his head, they were both breathing heavily.

"I've missed kissing you," Murdo said. "I never thought I'd miss kissing above all other activities."

The carriage took a deep bend then, throwing them against one another and making them laugh, even as David's leg ached like the very devil. When they came out of the bend, Murdo said, "Look, you can see Laverock House from here."

He pointed out the window, and David followed the line of his arm to a house several miles away, set on a hillside, looking down over Murdo's land. It was difficult to make much out from this distance, but it looked to be a good-sized manor house, built of solid grey stone.

"Your home," Murdo said. "For the next few months."

Home.

It sounded good.

It sounded…wonderful.

David looked up to find Murdo smiling at him, and he smiled back.

He was going home.

And it felt right.

THE END

Read the next instalment of David and Murdo's story in Book Three of the Enlightenment series, *Enlightened*

ENLIGHTENED

David Lauriston has been recuperating at Lord Murdo Balfour's Laverock estate for the last five months. At Laverock, he has regained his health and confidence and has found—with Murdo—more happiness and contentment than he has never known before.

David is all too aware that some day soon he will have to leave Laverock—and Murdo—and return to his legal practice in Edinburgh, just as Murdo will have to return to his life in London. But when David's mentor, Patrick Chalmers, asks David to return to Edinburgh to visit him on his deathbed, it seems that day has come sooner than either David or Murdo would have wished.

Chalmers begs David to undertake one last piece of business for him: to secure the future of Chalmers's daughter Elizabeth. But to carry out his old mentor's wishes, David must travel to London, with Murdo.

No sooner have the two men arrived in the capital than they encounter Murdo's ruthlessly manipulative father, who reveals a shocking secret that rocks David to his foundations. What's more, when David discovers Elizabeth is facing far greater danger than even her father feared, he is determined to help her, no matter the cost to his own safety.

As the stakes rise, it is Murdo who must choose what he is prepared to sacrifice to keep David at his side, and ask whether there is any possibility of lasting happiness for men like them.

Book One of the Enlightenment Series, *Provoked*

PROVOKED

Tormented by his forbidden desires for other men and the painful memories of the childhood friend he once loved, lawyer David Lauriston tries to maintain a celibate existence while he forges his reputation in Edinburgh's privileged legal world.

But then, into his repressed and orderly life, bursts Lord Murdo Balfour.

Cynical, hedonistic and utterly unapologetic, Murdo could not be less like David. And as appalled as David is by Murdo's unrepentant self-interest, he cannot resist the man's sway. Murdo tempts and provokes David in equal measure, forcing him to acknowledge his physical desires.

But Murdo is not the only man distracting David from his work. Euan MacLennan, the brother of a convicted radical David once represented, approaches David to beg him for help. Euan is searching for the government agent who sent his brother to Australia on a convict ship, and other radicals to the gallows. Despite knowing it may damage his career, David cannot turn Euan away.

As their search progresses, it begins to look as though the trail may lead to none other than Lord Murdo Balfour, and David has to wonder whether it's possible Murdo could be more than he seems. Is he really just a bored aristocrat, amusing himself at David's expense, or could he be the agent provocateur responsible for the fate of Peter MacLennan and the other radicals?

Thank you for taking the time to read this story—I do hope you enjoyed it. I'm very appreciative of any reviews—good or bad—that readers are kind enough to take the time to post, whether at retailer sites, on social media or on blogs or reviews.

If you want to sign up for my newsletter, you can do that on my website, where you can also find out more about my books. If you want to connect with me, you can do that on Twitter, Facebook and Goodreads.

Website: www.joannachambers.com
Twitter: @ChambersJoanna
Facebook: facebook.com/joanna.chambers.58

Titles by Joanna Chambers

The Enlightenment Series
Provoked
Beguiled
Enlightened
Seasons Pass
Unnatural

Porthkennack Series (Riptide)
A Gathering Storm

Other novel length titles
The Dream Alchemist
Unforgivable
The Lady's Secret

Novellas and Short Stories
Humbug (a Christmas tale)
Rest and Be Thankful
(appeared in the *Comfort and Joy* anthology)
Introducing Mr. Winterbourne
(appeared in the *Another Place in Time* anthology)
Mr. Perfect's Christmas
(appeared in the *Wish Come True* anthology)

Made in the USA
Middletown, DE
17 June 2020